CW00515005

Hard Cargo

Necrospace, Volume 6

Sean-Michael Argo

Published by Sean-Michael Argo, 2023.

HARD CARGO
Necrospace Book VI

By Sean-Michael Argo

Also by Sean-Michael Argo

Beautiful Resistance
Defiance Pattern
Opposition Shift
Significant Contact

Extinction Fleet
Space Marine Ajax
Space Marine Loki
Space Marine Apocalypse

Necrospace
Salvage Marines
Dead Worlds
Trade War
Ghost Faction
Carrion Duty
Hard Cargo

Starwing Elite
Attack Ships
Ghost Fleet
Alpha Lance

Standalone
War Machines
DinoMechs: Battle Force Jurassic

Edited by TL Bland

TABLE OF CONTENTS

Prologue

PROLOGUE

It is the Age of The Corporation.

The common man toils under the watchful eye of the elite and their enforcers. The rules of law have long been replaced by the politics of profit. For many centuries, the Covenants of Commerce have ruled mankind, from boardroom to factory floor, from mine deep to fertile field, upon the battlefields of heart, of mind, and of distant star.

The dark ages of feudalism have returned with capitalistic ferocity. There is no peace among the stars of mapped space; business is booming.

Impoverished workers drown in debt, laboring for subsistence pay. Mercenaries of every kind wage war, loyal to the banner of any company willing to meet their price. Everyone in existence is locked in a ceaseless struggle for economic dominance and survival. Scavengers and space pirates swoop in to loot what they can from the forgotten and unprotected.

To be a human being in such times is to be one among countless billions in a civilization spread across a vast universe, all ensnared in the same blood-soaked web of capitalism, most doomed to be ground to dust amidst the gears of progress.

There are some people, however, those rare few, who rise from the ranks of the faceless masses, to make their mark upon history.

This is one such tale.

NO REST

A caustic wind blew through his soul as the undead machine reached out for him and everything went black.

The first thing he noticed was her smell, the delicate aroma washing over his senses and drawing him from sleep, raising him up from the depths of some dark place and into awareness. Shadows receded, and ghosts faded away as her hands moved gently across his chest, over countless scars of battles won and lost, and then guided him into her gentle warmth. Her hair cascaded across his face as she leaned over to draw him in closer. As her lips met his, he found the strength to surge upwards despite the pain of his wounds. Their bodies wound together upon the soft sheets, like mating snakes rolling through fallen leaves, and together, they knew a boundless joy.

The nature of such moments is that they fade, and as Samuel lay on his back, with Sura's head resting upon his chest, he felt the dull pain in his body begin to flare into something more robust. He did not want the moment to end, and fought against it, gritting his teeth against the sharp edges of agony.

Doc Rayburn had saved the marine's life, but the field surgery had been a crude one, and the healing somewhat haphazard. He had a weak tea that Doc made from some of the leaves that grew locally, but there was little in the way of pharmaceutical painkillers beyond the handful that Doc had given him shortly after Samuel had awakened on the bloody grass of the clearing.

Samuel focused on the lock of dark hair that lay across Sura's face, watching it flutter back and forth as her sleeping breath moved through it. They hadn't been able to keep their hands off each other in the week since Samuel and the other Longstriders had fought the Tasca slavers, and though they were as careful as lovers could be, the continued activity came with a cost. The two bullet wounds in Samuel's side were positively screaming now, the electric sting of nerve endings howling for the marine to adjust his position. He could lay on his side, but that would mean letting the moment go, and Samuel wanted every second of it he could seize.

The two of them had fought through lonely years and countless enemies to make their life together and then had been forced to continue fighting. The pain in his side was a brutal reminder of the endless struggle that was his life, Sura's life, and their son's life.

As his thoughts drifted to Orion, his gaze drifted around the small bedroom of the cabin he and Sura had built together. He realized that the dawn light was only now peeking through the window.

The boy would still be asleep, thought Samuel, before considering that soon he would no longer be able to think in those terms. Orion was on the cusp of young adulthood, and soon he would begin his own struggle to find life and identity in this vast scrapyard of a universe.

The sound of movement outside the door caught Samuel's attention, and he could hear his son making his best attempts at being quiet as he prepared for the outdoors. Cragg, the saurian companion that had been with Orion since hatching, made a soft clicking sound with its claws as it moved across the short hallway from Orion's bedroom and into the main cabin.

The sound of a rifle's slide racking, the chambering of a round, told Samuel that Orion was leaving for a grok hunt. The quadrupeds were most active in the dawn hours, and the flesh of one of them would feed the family, and Cragg, for several weeks if Orion was able to take one. They were cunning creatures, silent and adept at camouflage. They were the prey of the large feline creatures that sometimes prowled the lonely forests of Longstride. Cragg's flesh was poisonous to the big cats, and so as long as the saurian was nearby, Orion would have little to fear from the planet's apex predator.

The thought of predators brought to mind the Tasca slavers once more and left Samuel faced with a decision he still had to make. In the last week the dreams had only gotten worse, and no matter how much love he made to his wife or how much of Doc's homemade tea he quaffed, the Gedra nightmare persisted. There had been something in one of the cryo-crates they'd offloaded from the Tasca ship, and though he lay wounded and dying, Samuel could hear it roaring in his mind. The other Longstriders felt it too, a sort of evil radiating from the crate. After opening all the others crates to set the people inside free, the large, menacing one had been left alone.

Doc had told Samuel they'd hauled it into the forest, just past Kovac's Ridge, and buried it. The Longstriders had destroyed the transponders on all the cryo-crates, except for the one with blackout plates welded onto the crate's viewports. They were going to affix several thermal charges and slag the cryo-crate, but before passing out, Samuel had apparently turned his head and looked at it. Both the pilot, Tanya, and Doc Rayburn had heard Samuel say "I know you" to the crate. Given the palpable energy coming off the thing, they had decided to leave it for Samuel to determine how to deal with it once he'd healed.

The truth was, Samuel had been avoiding making this decision for the last several days. If he was well enough to be with his wife, even if it cost him tremendous pain afterward, then he could take the skiff out past the ridge. Though Samuel was loath to bring him, Orion was becoming a solid driver, and the marine would need the boy's help to dig up the crate. Samuel wasn't sure what he would do once he had unearthed it, but he knew it was time to make the journey.

The moment had passed, Samuel realized as he looked down to meet Sura's open eyes. He had no idea how long she'd been watching him, but from the expression on her face, it was clear she knew what he was thinking.

"Whatever is in that crate isn't just buried, Samuel," Sura said in a small voice, gentle, but firm, "It is waiting for you."

"I keep having the Gedra dream, and I know there's more to it than trade war PTSD," responded Samuel as he winced from the pain of both he and Sura shifting their positions ever so slightly. "I think I've been avoiding it."

"We do what needs to be done, husband. We are Longstriders now." Sura moved a hand up to cup Samuel's face. "And before that, we were Grotto born and raised. Facing things, getting on with it, is in our blood."

"Fair point, wife," said Samuel, with a grim smile. "Even in our most tender moments, there is steel in our spine. Well, mine, at least."

"Who are you and what have you done with my marine?" laughed Sura with a theatrical flair as she framed the question. "I do believe you just made a joke, and that is a far cry from the brooding boy I met outside the Enforcer's Spire."

"Getting shot and getting laid all in the same week does things to a man," smirked Samuel as he gripped Sura's thigh, inviting her to slide the rest of the way up his body to straddle him. "When Orion gets back from the hunt I'll dose on Rayburn's tea and take the skiff."

"The world might change again," breathed Sura before she kissed Samuel deeply and began to move her hips against his, the pleasure of her upon him balancing out the toll it cost him in pain, "Depending on what you find there."

"Then let's make the most of the dawn while we have it," whispered Samuel as he gripped Sura's waist, the rush of hormones already pushing the pain out of his consciousness and filtering out everything but the woman on top of him.

Hours later Samuel breathed deeply of the moist forest air and was happy that he got his lungs full without a lance of pain stopping him short. Doc's tea was perhaps stronger than he'd given it credit for, thought Samuel, as he took some small pleasure in how fresh and clean the air was on this tiny planet. With no industry to speak of, beyond the homesteading of the locals, there was nothing to befoul the pristine natural landscape. That was why Sura had picked this place, and Samuel felt that there could be no more perfect home in the universe.

He turned his head and looked at Orion as the boy skillfully piloted the small skiff over the land.

Orion was still in his hunting kit, which was a patchwork body glove made out of leather and ceramic plates, carefully crafted to give maximum mobility with modest protection from thorn, tooth, and claw. It was still a little big for him, but he'd soon fill it out well.

Though the boy had been born in the grinding industrial society of Grotto and had spent his early years in the cramped living quarters of corporate housing, space stations, and starships, he had blossomed in the rugged environment of Longstride. It was amazing what open air and clean food could do for a child. Samuel felt a surge of pride as he watched the youngster deftly maneuver around the large trees and massive moss-covered boulders that covered the forest floor.

Sura had insisted that Orion accompany Samuel on this journey, and though she declared that it was so the marine wouldn't have to overexert himself, Samuel knew it was more for Orion's benefit. Riding with the marine to unearth something that was sure to be trouble, carried a risk that none of them could ignore. Samuel himself was fully suited in his Reaper armor and cradled his combat rifle with deadly purpose. In fact, it was when she had seen the marine preparing himself for possible violence that Sura had encouraged Orion's participation.

Samuel knew what she was doing, and though it darkened his thoughts to consider, he found himself in reluctant agreement. Sura had been forced to become a different person when Helion troops attacked Pier 16. She had fled with Orion and found a place on the freelance, ink-rock prospector ship, *Rig Halo* as a refugee, though by the time she stepped off the ship she'd been transformed into a warrior and ink-rocker herself. Through the many hardships of life in necrospace, Sura had fought her own war even as Samuel endured his on the Ellisian front. The assault by the Tasca slavers had rattled everyone, and Sura clearly wanted her son to take a step towards being prepared for the larger and much more grim reality that lurked beyond the boundaries of their forest paradise.

Orion was scared, that was easy to tell, like any child would be, though he was excited too, and in that excitement, Samuel could almost see the man that his son might one day become.

The boy had been a baby while on Grotto and a toddler on Pier 16. It was aboard the *Rig* that his mind had begun to take shape, amidst the rough crowd of laborers, adventurers, and outcasts that comprised the *Halo's* crew. His most formative years had been here, on Longstride, where he'd learned to build, to hunt, to grow, and to fend for himself just as much as his family. Orion was old enough his mind had begun to thirst for knowledge, yearning for experience beyond the green world and his parent's homestead.

In the settlement, there were girls aplenty to turn the head of any boy, and Samuel had seen the spark in Orion's eyes at the last festival, but this was something different. It was that same glimmer the boy's eyes had when his father would tell him tales of the mighty ganger, Vol, or the mercenary mystic, Imago, the daring of Reaper Ben Takeda, and countless other tales from Samuel's Reaper life. Stories wiped clean of the blood and misery, given the shine of heroism and adventure. Orion knew there was more to it now, and he was hungry for that truth.

They were wearing armor and carrying weapons, moving through the woods for no festival or hunt, but to unearth some piece of a distant war. Or not so distant, Samuel reminded himself, as he ejected the combat rifle's magazine and re-slotted it, an old habit from his early days as a salvage marine. There was violence in the air, and the memory of firefights and lost comrades were as fresh as the wind. It had only been a week since the fight with the Tasca, and though Tanya had done her best to field strip and clean the Reaper armor, Samuel could see traces of blood and smears of gun grease on parts of the interlocking plates that protected his body. The pilot had done her best, but she was no marine.

Nor was Orion, thought Samuel, feeling guilty for a brief moment that he'd agreed to bring the boy. He then recalled his last sight of Sura as the skiff had pulled away when he'd left to fight the slavers. She'd been standing on the porch, her hair falling across her shoulders, face delicate and beautiful, but her eyes as hard as the metal of Vol's heavy revolver, strapped to her thigh. Sura had learned how to survive, how to fight back, to protect what was hers, and Samuel knew it was high time Orion began his own education in that regard.

"One minute out," said Samuel as he pointed towards a cluster of trees just across a stream that they were rapidly approaching. "Set us down over there, we make the final approach on foot."

"Yes sir," responded Orion, his voice the awkward mix of high and low tones that boys of his age possessed, as he guided the skiff around a boulder and down the slope towards the tree cluster.

The skiff was small, only large enough for two passengers and a modest amount of gear, which in this case was a force-shovel and Cragg. The vehicle, which hovered several feet off the ground, smoothly eased to a stop just at the trees, and then gently lowered itself onto landing stabilizers as Orion shut the turbines down.

Samuel dismounted the vehicle and made a security sweep of the area moving in a tight circle. He came around to Orion's side, holding the skiff steady as his son clambered out and got his rifle ready. Cragg leaped out of his perch onto the loamy ground.

Samuel turned to Orion as he held his combat rifle in the ready position, making a display of disengaging the safety.

"If I move, you move. If I stop, you stop. If I shoot, you shoot," said Samuel flatly, easily falling back into his squad leader's demeanor as if it had not been half a decade or more since he'd been an active duty marine. "Copy?"

"Um, yes, sir," stammered Orion for a moment, visibly shaken by the sight of his father's helmeted face and armored body, as if only now realizing how real this story had become. "I mean, copy."

Samuel gave his son a curt nod and turned to march deeper into the woods, flanked by Cragg as the saurian joined them. It was easy to see the disturbed earth where the other Longstriders had unloaded a digger from their cargo skiff, and as the marine approached he could tell just how hastily it was all done. They hadn't tried to cover their tracks, which was just as well since they'd told him where to go, but it was clear from how badly they tore up the terrain that everyone had been in a rush. He did not blame them, as the entire area pulsed with menace, and as Samuel walked onwards he noticed how the saurian grew more and more agitated.

The trio crested the ridge after another five minutes of trudging through the underbrush, following the crude trail hacked out by the heavy machinery used to deposit the cryo-crate. Below them, Samuel could, at last, see where the crate had been buried. The frontier folk had used an agri-class force shovel, likely mounted to one of their skiffs, to tear a vast chunk of rock and dirt out of the land. From the ruts in the ground, it looked as if they'd shove the crate into the crater and then, perhaps not so gently, released the field on the shovel and allowed all of that earth to fall back down into the massive hole. The entire process, while crude, would have taken only moments.

Cragg hissed with aggression and what, to Samuel seemed like fear as the saurian moved in a wide circle around the crater. While the sauropod was unwilling to go further it also appeared unwilling to turn its back on the area. Samuel swept his eyes across the area, and after deciding that there weren't any unwanted eyes watching them, he moved forward. Once he was right at the edge of the crater, the feeling of menace felt like a gale force wind blowing against his mind, and as he looked at Orion, he saw that the boy could feel it too. He suspected, however, that others, including his son, did not feel it quite as potently as he did. Orion was uncomfortable and knew he was in the presence of something that could only be described as evil, and yet Samuel could tell it was not pushing against the boy's psyche the way it was for him.

It was almost a voice to Samuel's perceptions, something just beneath the surface of his consciousness, calling out to him. Or screaming at him, thought the marine as he took note of how the moss and lesser vegetation inside the crater's boundary had already begun to wither and die. Corruption and madness radiated from whatever was down there inside the crate, and now that he was so close, Samuel's suspicions about what he had to do were growing.

"Bring up the shovel," said Samuel without turning around, gesturing with the muzzle of his rifle at a patch of dying moss covered with dirt just inside the crater area, and Orion slung the solo-class device from his shoulder. "Start there," Samuel directed pointing at the spot. "Take it slow, just like you're digging an irrigation trench. The others took a big risk just dropping tons of dirt and rock on this thing. If they breached containment we might have to shoot something."

The boy's face went pale with fear for a moment, and he did not move, until Samuel turned his face towards him and spoke.

"I'm doing good to stand, son, but I can still shoot," he assured the boy as he tapped his trigger finger against the flat metal above the firing mechanism of his combat rifle. "Dig it out carefully, and if something down there gets loose, I'll drop it."

"If something bad is down there can't we just leave it alone?" asked Orion despite the fact that he moved forward and activated the force shovel as instructed.

"Slavers brought this thing to our doorstep, and instead of slagging it, Doc and the others left it up to us," answered Samuel, "If there's anything I've learned about the Gedra it's that they don't stay buried. Sooner or later someone will have to engage."

Orion swallowed, and then turned towards the crater. He stood silently for a moment before pointing the force hammer at the ground and squeezing the trigger. The tool was a smaller version of the device that had created the crater, a two-meter-long telescoping shaft that had two repulsors mounted on one end on either side of the wide shovel spade. Orion thrust it into the spongy soil and then heaved it up and out. As he did the repulsors lifted large amounts of soil and even a few large stones, the pattern of the energy field following the shape of the spade from which it emitted. Orion hurled the load aside and went back for a second, and then a third. Within a few minutes, he'd already moved enough dirt and rock to equal an hour or more of standard digging.

The work was good for Orion, thought Samuel as he divided his attention from observing his son and watching the treeline, to distract his mind at least somewhat from the horror that no doubt lay in wait underneath the rock and soil. The marine wasn't sure exactly what he was looking for out there in the trees, beyond pulling basic security, though he felt it important to do none the less. It was as if he felt hunted, an intent out there beyond his perception, and he couldn't shake the feeling. More than likely there was a feline predator somewhere in the underbrush, watching them hungrily despite the presence of Cragg as a deterrent.

As Orion continued his work, Samuel began to feel what he could conceptualize only as a kind of dark energy emanating from the ground below.

"You're close to it now," said Samuel as the young man dumped another mound of dirt and rock, "One more full load and then power down, we'll dig the rest out cold, don't want to damage the crate."

Orion nodded and gingerly pulled up one last shovelful, and after he deposited it he thumbed off the activator, making his tool as inert as any other shovel.

It had been a rather large investment, Samuel found himself thinking, but the force shovel had paid for itself on the homestead, making the work of several people possible by an individual in a fraction of the time. Now, however, they needed to proceed with more caution, more precision. He was loath to allow Orion any closer to whatever was down there, but it had to be done.

Orion moved around the rather large hole he'd made and began using the shovel to move smaller pieces of rock and clumps of dirt. After a few minutes, the outline of the crate began to take shape, and Samuel could see that Orion felt at least a little of what was radiating from inside. Samuel slung his rifle, moving carefully down into the hole, then put his hand on the boy's shoulder.

"I'll take it from here," said Samuel. He could tell the youngster wanted to stay and help, but the relief on Orion's face was clear. "Take overwatch. We're out in the open here, might as well keep a rifle at the ready."

Cragg hissed in agitation as it continued to circle the crater, not daring to cross the perimeter to join the two humans at the center of it.

Orion climbed out and took up a position just at the edge of the crater, where the land was slightly more elevated, giving him a better vantage point over the clearing. Samuel was happy that Orion's hunting experience gave him those kinds of instincts, to automatically seek the best firing position as he understood it. Things were different once a gunfight got started, but such lessons were hard learned through experience, and Samuel genuinely hoped his son would never know the chaos and fury of such a thing.

Samuel missed the rush of a good firefight, how time slowed to a glacial pace even as the heat of battle made a volcano in the soul of everyone involved and hated that he felt so. It seemed that no matter how far he ran, there was always a fight to be had, and some part of him was happy for it. His thoughts were a jumble as Samuel ran his armored hands across the surface of the crate, pushing away the last few inches of dirt that covered the top of it. He felt comfortable here, in this realm of danger and violence, more than he did in his garden or even in Sura's arms and admitting that to himself came with a cost.

A caustic wind blew through his soul as the undead machine reached out for him.

Samuel had felt the psychic lash of the Gedra before, in the presence of the Alpha cyborgs, and yet this was something more. He felt the throb of the crate, a physical hum, and shiver of the metal struggling to contain an expanding force that reminded Samuel of the reinforced disposal domes used to detonate enemy ordinance.

The cryo-crate was just a casing, an outer sleeve as it were, for some kind of containment unit hidden behind the blackout plates. There was a Gedra beast behind that metal, though something more terrible and powerful than even the Alpha cyborgs, and that alone was horrifying enough. Samuel's tongue tasted the bite of electricity, and an all too familiar wind blew through his mind, making him wonder how his body could feel it through the armor.

Grotto Command was certain that the Alpha cyborgs, despite their tremendous capabilities and influence over the lesser Gedra beings, were not at the apex of the machine race. They were too specialized as grave guardians to be anything else. Someone or something had built those dead cities and occupied the bleached, scorched, and desiccated worlds on the other side of the Ellisian Line.

As the psychic waves crashed into Samuel, he began to put the pieces together. The Tasca had operatives pillaging the battlefields of the Ellisian trade war, so were working regularly across the Line. Clearly, they had gotten their hands on this nightmare, whatever it was, either by unearthing it themselves or more likely stealing it from someone else. The direct routes back into mapped space were, even now, choked with corporate traffic, much of it military, and no criminal would dare move that way. They would take the ghost lanes through corporate space, long stretches of empty space where the hope of rescue was as slim as the chance of encountering traffic.

Red list ships and Reaper tugs used them often, as most space salvage ended up in those lonely places. As Samuel thought it out, pulling up star charts in his mind's eye even as the panic started to build in the back of his brain, he considered it likely that the Tasca cutter was attempting to reach either a Praxis Mundi outpost or one of the Augur research stations. There was nothing else out here on the frontier, except for a few pioneer communities, which turned out to be targets too juicy for the slavers to pass up.

Samuel realized that it was simple human greed that had forced this monster into his life. If the slavers had just gone about their business and completed their run without raiding Longstride, so much would be different. Men and women who were not dead would be working their homesteads, just like Samuel would be, raising his family and worrying more about Orion finding a girl at festival than preparing him for a fight. He'd thought when a Tasca operative gunned down Spencer Green, his friend, and fellow marine, that they couldn't take anything more from him. The slavers would not leave well enough alone, and now Samuel found himself crouching atop a cryo-crate containing some kind of Gedra tomb lord. Whatever this thing was, it had more power than any Alpha cyborg, and it had to be the containment unit within the crate that kept its psychic lash from having more bite than it already did.

The marine swept away the last of the dirt to reveal the blackout plates that covered the cryo-crate, and as if those last bits of soil were holding back the presence within the energy surged through him.

Something hardened in Samuel then, a wound finally turning to scar, as he understood what he had to do.

Necrospace would never let him go, of that he was now certain. He was ashamed of his excitement and emboldened by his anger. Samuel roared in fury and ecstasy as he took a knee and slammed his fist into the blackout plate position where the occupant's head would be.

"This is the job!" he roared through his tears at the crate, at the beast beneath within, at the universe itself.

He pounded his fist into the plate over and over, the armored knuckles of his glove making only the slightest scratch upon the reinforced metal.

"This is the job!"

PROSPECTORS

The engines of a starship could be heard in the distance, the sound of them filling the usually serene valley forest and causing flocks of birds to take flight.

It was a transitional period for the environment when the last vestiges of autumn were giving way to the first tinges of winter cold. The evergreens and ferns were wet with the heavy fog that had blanketed the valley before morning light had driven it away. Samuel could see darting shapes of grok rushing through the underbrush just inside the distant treeline.

Moments later the prospector ship *Rig Halo* dropped out of the low hanging clouds, like a comet falling from the sky to disturb the peace of what had been known as Hyst Valley to the locals of Longstride.

Samuel watched as the ship's landing thrusters burned through the gently flowing grass of the modest clearing in which the Hyst family had built their home. Seconds later the support struts of the *Halo* tore great gouts in the soil as the starship completed its landing. The valley floor shook from the impact, which was less than the marine would have expected from such a vessel. While the *Rig* had been heavily modified with recon and combat capabilities, it was still at its core a rugged mining vessel, and no matter how many sleek armored veins and weapons arrays the crew put on it the beast would always be an ugly workhorse.

Samuel begrudgingly admitted he liked that about the *Halo*, and even as the ship had now come to symbolize everything he hated about his family's predicament, the patchwork face of it reminded him of Tango Platoon. The Rig wasn't that much different from the scrap wagons that Samuel and his fellow marines had built years ago to plow through the debris fields left by ship-to-ship void battles, or the armored speedboats they'd built to navigate the brackenworlds. Seeing the ship begin to power down, hull still smoldering from breaking orbit and descending through the clouds gave Samuel cause to sweep his gaze across the homestead that they would very soon be leaving.

Samuel took in the sight of their garden, a patch of earth brimming with fall squash and root vegetables. For a man and woman of Grotto to grow their own food from dirt that they owned was a rare thing indeed, in fact, unheard of in Samuel's experience. There were a few people in the stacks who had a potted plant or two, but those were always weak and sickly things that did not thrive on recycled air and processed nutrients. He looked upon his workshop, a small building made of fab-planks in which he and Orion kept their skiff in working order, and where recently he'd found it necessary to patch and polish his combat armor.

The thought of violence made his eyes shift to the cabin, that icon of frontier freedom for which he and Sura, and Orion for that matter, had sacrificed so much to possess. It was a small thing in actual size, but for the former Grotto citizens, so used to living in the cramped hab-stacks of Baen 6, it had been a veritable palace.

Sura's hand found his and squeezed.

Samuel turned his head and looked at his wife. He saw the streaks of tears on her cheek. As she used her other hand to wipe them clear he knew she was seeing their valley just as he was. Beside her stood Orion, and though he'd been shaken mightily by the trip to the crate's burial site and his father's subsequent outburst, the boy was visibly excited. Even after the forest, despite his fear, Orion had asked to accompany Samuel into the village, and onwards to the Praxis outpost if Samuel was able to find a bush pilot willing to make the trip. Samuel had refused, insisting the boy stay home, though when the marine returned from his journey, the news that *Rig Halo* was inbound had perked the youngster up considerably. For Orion, the sight of the *Halo* was the beginning of a grand adventure, even if for his parents it was the end of a fleeting dream.

"It was beautiful while it lasted, Samuel," whispered Sura as she squeezed Samuel's hand once more and looked him directly in the eyes. "No matter what happens, remember that. For a time, we had this, and nothing can take that from us."

Samuel was about to speak, unsure of what to say but knowing she wanted his affirmation when the hatch of the *Rig Halo* hissed loudly as it opened. Sura turned her head at the sound, and from the way her expression changed, ever so subtly, from grief to something close to warmth, Samuel knew that Kelkis Dar was disembarking. The marine turned to look at the *Rig* and sure enough, he saw the spirited captain of the prospector ship marching down the gangplank.

Behind him came a grim man wearing a patchwork set of Helion battle armor, the sight of which set Samuel's teeth on edge out of habit. The man was no doubt the ship's security chief, with two of his hired guns walking side by side behind him. They were all armed, which made Samuel glad, as it meant that Dar had taken the marine's assessment of the situation seriously.

It stung to see Sura react to Dar's presence, though Samuel had long known that she and the captain had once entertained feelings for one another. That had been years ago, and they'd never acted on them, but it stung all the same. Especially now that the captain and his ship represented the Hyst family's best hope for survival and escape. Samuel took a deep breath and did his best to let those thoughts go, shaking the past from his mind even as he tried not to think about the homestead they were about to leave as well.

"The Hyst family calls and the *Rig Halo* answers," smiled Dar as he swept his arms wide. The man's flair for dramatics ran counter to the more reserved cultural tendencies of the former Grotto citizens, a character trait of the captain that Samuel found grating.

Orion however, did not share the same feeling, and happily stepped forward to bump his fist against Dar's as he crossed his legs, bending at the knees slightly to perform a swordsman's bow. The movement was mirrored by Dar, who had taught it to the boy when Orion and Sura were on their own, while Samuel was embedded in the Ellisian trade war. It was a customary greeting aboard the *Halo*, also in common use among space pirates, which as far as Samuel was concerned, described the crew of the *Rig Halo* in everything but name.

"What have they been feeding you?" laughed Dar as he clamped his hands against Orion's shoulders. "I'd wager if you were on Baen 6 right now you'd be the biggest kid in the stacks!"

Samuel bristled at the captain's familiarity but did his best not to let it show. Dar had saved Sura and Orion from the massacre on Pier 16, and in spite of his obvious desires and reputation as lady's man, he'd never pressed Sura. They'd lived aboard his ship and served on the crew for several years without incident, and the marine had to remind himself of that.

Dar and the crew were taking a significant risk in coming here. Samuel had offered them everything he and Sura had, but he knew full well that their money wasn't nearly enough to cover the potential risks involved in bringing them aboard. Captain Dar was once again snatching the Hysts from the jaws of doom, and Samuel respected that, was grateful for it, even if his emotions surged and his pride burned.

Samuel was partially thankful that the man in the Helion armor stepped directly in front of him, looking the homesteader up and down. The silent confrontation gave him something to focus his attention on instead of the way that Sura embraced the captain when Dar moved from Orion to greet her.

The man in front of Samuel was slightly taller than the homesteader, and the plates of body armor gave him a broad presence that could not be ignored. Neither could the stout mechanical left arm which cradled the well-worn Helion rifle and though it reminded Samuel of Boss Taggart's mechanical appendage, the limb was clearly of a finer make.

It was difficult to be this close to that much hardware from a corporation that had been his enemy for so many years, though not nearly so much as it was to count the seconds that Sura held the captain before finally letting him step away and adjust his coat.

"So, this is the Reaper, eh?" scoffed the armored man as he flexed his fingers around the grip of his rifle, his thick Helion accent giving his words a gravelly tone. "They had us believing that all you Tango Platoon grunts were actually Merchants Militant in disguise, some kind of propaganda stunt to make salvage marines seem like more than just low rent scrappers."

"Narek, back off!" snapped Dar as he turned from Sura and glared at his security chief, his face a flash of anger over the botched moment of reunion.

"I'm just saying he looks like a regular guy is all," grumbled the Helion man as he took a step backward and waved his mechanical hand in a gesture of begrudging acceptance. The muzzle of his rifle drifted ever so slightly in Samuel's direction as his stance shifted to support the movement. "Plenty of folks in the verse who can pull a trigger and work a torch. People who don't have to buy into our license under the table. Trying to ghost out of here like they are, maybe there's a reward that's worth more than their buy-in."

The armored man's eyes glittered as he spoke, and Samuel recognized the look, feeling as if he had it in his own eyes at that moment. The Ellisian trade war was a long time ago, but for the men and women who'd fought through it, the flood of memories was on a hair trigger.

Samuel could see the service decals, faded though they were, emblazoned on the man's shoulder piece. That armor had seen duty across the Ellisian Line, showing three different grey octagonal symbols that Samuel knew represented Gedra tomb world campaigns. Samuel also recognized two red triangles with a series of circles and hatch marks, and though he did not know which specific engagements they might refer too, he did know that they represented battles with Grotto forces. From the way Narek wore the armor, Samuel guessed that it belonged to the man, and if that was the case, the homesteader was standing in front of a Helion battle trooper. All of a sudden, the old war felt fresh as ever, and Samuel felt his hand stray to hover just above the grip of his combo revolver where it rested in a thigh holster.

He might be a former Reaper, but being a marine was for life, and it took everything Samuel had not to escalate.

"Captain, with all due respect," hissed Samuel through gritted teeth as he willfully kept his hand off of his weapon, breathing in and out slowly as he worked to calm himself, to overcome the innate desire to fight an old enemy, "Your man here is damaging my calm."

"Stand down, gentlemen," commanded Dar as he stepped towards the two men with hands resting on the handles of his sword and pistol. His tall frame and wind-whipped cape added a weight to his words that caught the attention of both Samuel and Narek, the captain being well versed in how to speak to military men.

"That war is over and happened on the other side of the universe. While I appreciate that no man can walk away from a protracted conflict like that without some baggage, this posturing is not solving anything. Your corporate affiliations no longer apply here, and I will not have members of my crew at each other's throats."

Samuel took a deep breath and slowly moved his hand away from his pistol as he briefly dipped his head in acknowledgment. Narek finally grunted and slid his rifle along its strap to put it in a carry position. Dar looked at each man for a moment longer then the security chief turned and walked back towards the *Rig*. Dar turned to the other two security crew that had been with Narek.

"They don't have much, but help Orion here see it to their quarters if you please," said Dar, his words sending the two men into action. They helped Orion load a small dolly skiff with the meager belongings of the Hyst family.

The captain turned fully towards Samuel and Sura, a tiny smile tugging at the edges of his mouth as he caught sight of Sura slipping a small holdout pistol back into the folds of her waistband.

"I apologize for Narek, he is a relatively new addition to the crew," said Dar as he adjusted his weapons and coat, more to occupy his hands than to fix any kind of disheveled appearance. "I found him on Cresseda, hellish place that little moon, essentially a series of bars and cheap hab-stacks that serve as a clearinghouse for non-union mercs, so he is still learning proper ship's decorum."

"I know things get violent sometimes," nodded Sura before she lifted her personal pack off the ground and pushed the hair that had fallen in front of her face behind her ear, a gesture which Samuel could not help but notice he and Dar both appeared fond of. "But why would the *Rig* need mercs on the crew?"

"The short answer is that necrospace is getting more dangerous, just like you've learned out here on the frontier," answered Dar, his expression darkening, as he gestured for the two homesteaders to walk with him towards their cabin, "The trade war and all of those new worlds across the Ellisian Line, dead as they may be, has had something of a ripple effect. The commodities markets are more volatile than ever, fortunes won and lost in the blink of an eye.

"Some organizations are flooding the market while others are trying to hoard and kickstart a shortage. We might pull an ocean's worth of ink-rock from a frontier world, fight off claim jumpers every step of the way because the juice is paying top rate, and by the time we get it to an exchange desk its worth less than what we spent to get it, only to be a fortune the next day after we sell it. Everyone is feeling the squeeze, from prospectors to even the registered factory planets. When you have no idea what your goods or labor are going to be worth tomorrow, you get fierce about the pay today."

"It's chaos out there and everyone has guns," growled Samuel as the trio came to stand at the bottom steps of the cabin that he and Sura had built together.

"On the button, Samuel, on the button," nodded Dar as he rested one arm on the pedestal that held up the porch, leaning on it so he could kick one leg out and affect a more casual pose. "Used to be we only had to fight for our scores on the rare occasion, but now there's enough competition it's worth the cost to keep a few trigger men full-time. Yanna hates it, says its only gotten worse since she started, and you know her, Sura, she's been with the *Rig* longer than even I have."

"Are you building up to a catch?" asked Samuel, suddenly feeling as if Dar wanted more than he'd indicated during their initial communications aboard the Praxis way station.

"No catch, just transparency, and I didn't want to scare you off, because the *Rig* is your best chance. You were shaken up when we spoke Samuel, cashing out and ghosting off a paradise like Longstride is a desperate move. I know you're tired of fighting." spoke Dar as he looked at the cabin, and then back to Sura, "You've both been fighting all your lives, for this slice of the good life. Whatever it is that you're running from, in order to leave this, I know it has to be as bad as it gets."

"I told you no disclosures," said Samuel, and Dar nodded.

"I don't want to know what's coming for you, Samuel. I gave you and Sura my word that you will have a place with us, no questions asked, but you have to know what you're getting into before you come aboard," insisted Dar as he slowly looked from the cabin to the still steaming hull of the *Rig Halo*, and then back to Sura specifically. "The line between being prospectors and being pirates has gotten blurred."

"So you got yourself some mercs because they're a necessary part of the process now," concluded Samuel, his voice low as he fought the urge to clench his fist. "You need men like Narek."

"Men like my husband," breathed Sura as her shoulders fell slightly, and Samuel could see her eyes begin to mist up.

"Everyone on the *Rig* knows how to shoot and fight, some better than others, but none of them are professional killers." Dar sighed as he looked at Samuel, then offered his hand to the homesteader. "You said you were ready to take up the torch for the *Rig*, and indeed we have much need of another skilled set of hands. But when the time comes, and I promise you it will, we're going to need your rifle too."

Samuel wanting nothing more than to draw his revolver and punch a hole in Dar's chest. The captain had assured him that the prospector license was the extent of their work. He'd experienced, briefly, life aboard the *Rig*, and Samuel knew he had to take the man at his word. There wasn't much choice in any of it, though Samuel had made it clear that he was not interested in being anyone's trigger man again. Dar had lied, but now that the captain had all of the Hyst's money, their belongings and even their son aboard the ship, there was little to be done about it. Samuel knew deep down that he was prepared to do anything to keep his family safe, and Dar knew that just as plainly, in fact, it appeared he was banking on it.

This is the job.

Samuel took Dar's hand and shook it, forging their bond even as he felt his connection to Hyst Valley cut to the quick. Not since he'd signed his contact in the Reaper recruitment office had he felt such a shift between the time now and the time that had come before. Sura's hand slid across his shoulder, and the marine felt a kind of strength returning to his limbs.

"Welcome to the *Rig Halo*," stated Captain Dar as he released Samuel's hand and then bowed to the couple before turning to walk towards the ship, "We dust off in five minutes."

Sura and Samuel stood quietly for a few moments, holding each other by the hand as they looked at their cabin. Soon the wind picked up and the *Rig*'s engines began to roar as the pilot started his takeoff procedure. Sura leaned in and kissed her man, then led him by the hand away from the cabin and towards the starship.

"Come on, Samuel," whispered Sura with a smile, the sort that was resilient and genuine even if weary from burden, a Grotto smile that the marine felt she'd always found a way to make beautiful.

"Let's go home."

TERMS OF AGREEMENT

"You know what my favorite thing about space travel is?" crackled the voice of Paul Lovat across the recovery channel.

The atmospheric interference and precipitation distorted the sound of it making it difficult to pick up on the nuance of the man's words. Trask had long ago accepted that when Lovat opened his mouth it was generally in an attempt at cheap humor. The lead enforcer chose not to respond and continued to scan the streets below as he toggled the ocular specs of his helmet in an attempt to adjust for the acid rain that fell in driving sheets. Perched as he was, atop one of the sturdier buildings in this wretched shantytown, he had a good vantage point for observing the primary thoroughfare of intersecting streets and alleyways below.

"No bad weather on a starship," continued Lovat, plunging ahead with his commentary despite the fact that neither Trask nor Aeomi had deigned to respond, something that was also a common occurrence. "Like my friends keep reminding me, no clouds stationside."

Trask finally gave a chuckle at the use of a common phrase thrown about by the table girls that Lovat usually spent most of his modest paycheck on in between enforcement actions. The young man at least had the stones to be open about his lifestyle, and Trask had to give him that.

Humor was not something the citizens of Grotto were known for, and neither was being particularly libertine when it came to sexuality and romance. Lovat was not the average Grotto man, however, and Trask supposed the job of enforcer took all kinds, so long as the job got done.

The veteran bond agent had to admit, as his wrist-mounted analytics pad chimed a gentle reminder that the acidity of the rain was only marginally within tolerable limits for human exposure, that he'd have preferred conducting a recovery stationside.

Trask looked over the area, taking in the full sight of the rain-soaked settlement simply known as Drill Post 47, in keeping with Grotto corporation's penchant for categorical simplicity when it came to naming people, places, and things.

The Post, as it was called by the locals, had been one of several boomtowns to spring up on this lonely planet, hanging in a wide orbit around a sun that was on its last billion years.

Freelance prospectors operating on a Grotto contract had discovered pockets of mordite gas underneath the rocky surface, sniffing it out with ground exploration instead of the orbital scans of the salaried surveyors who had already passed over the planet decades before. Grotto corporation immediately raised a mining colony expedition and sent several thousand settlers along with all the equipment they'd needed to exploit the gas. The corporation opened up private contracts, and sold claims to anyone willing to pay, so while Grotto natives mined what they could multitudes of other would-be colonists from across corporate space flocked to the planet hoping to make a quick fortune.

Trask had to give it to those original settlers, several generations prior, for making the most of what they brought with them. Being so far from the conventional trading routes meant that new lanes had to be charted, and for the most part the only traffic on or off the planet, or this single planet solar system in general, was to move gas out of the colony and supplies into it.

Trask looked down at entire multi-story buildings created from the shipping containers that had originally brought materials and equipment to the planet. Now they had been converted into crude hab-stacks, though the metal was beginning to show its age as the constant acid rain ate away at its thick hide.

There was no planning to the settlement, Trask reminded himself as he took in the sight of a dead end street that was blocked off by what appeared to be a tent encampment. On his own home of Uralisk

9 there would be no such haphazard squatting allowed, no obstruction of the flow of human and material traffic tolerated, and the homeless rounded up for work details or eventual penal assignment.

He could see the last vestiges of the wealth that had once flowed through this place. There were advanced personal vehicles in the streets, though most of them were now non-functional and had been converted to storefronts, emergency rain shelters, or stripped out for parts and abandoned. Vending machines offered a menagerie of delights, most of them now broken or powered down.

Trask could see, in the distance, an elevated slab of rock jutting up from the surface, upon which lay the once busy Alpha class starport. He could tell it was abandoned, or at least had been transformed from a starport into something else, as he noticed many dozens of flickering lights, giving him the impression that perhaps it was now just a giant structure in which those too impoverished to afford housing even on this sad rock would go to seek shelter.

The small planet was on the edge of Grotto territory, with everything past it being uncharted darkness or full necrospace. While it was spared the complications of sharing a border with Helion like the Grotto planets on the opposite side of the corporate empire, when the gas pockets were depleted so was Grotto's concern for the community there.

Trask shook his head, both to clear his visor of the caustic rain but also a reaction to his mental review of the bond recovery file he and his team had been issued some weeks ago.

Drill Post 47 was functionally abandoned, and the only reason there was still some modicum of trade traffic in this place was the modest production of one remaining mordite play. That one play did enough business to keep The Post alive, though for how long remained to be seen. From what Trask was able to glean in the first day on this miserable world was that the play itself was controlled by a criminal element.

Trask put the troubles of the boomtown gone bust from his mind. This was still Grotto space, and there was an enforcer's spire visible on the other end of the settlement. Local law enforcement could handle governing this place, and in fact, if his time as an enforcer on Uralisk 9 had taught him anything, it was that the law and the outlaw often worked hand in hand to maintain order. Some amount of corruption was inevitable and arguably necessary in keeping the peace. Bond Recovery Agent Jared Trask was not here to fight crime, he was here to maintain the functionality of Grotto society as a whole. As far as he was concerned the enforcers were better off staying out of his way.

"Boss, I have them," chimed the lilting voice of Aeomi, snapping Trask out of his reverie as he turned his head to look at his subordinate's position down in the streets below, "They moved right past me. Hard to catch the scent at distance because of this damn rain."

"I'm looking but I don't see them," responded Trask as his oculars zoomed in on Aeomi's position.

His hardware revealed a young woman dressed in a large overcoat to hide her body armor, holding an umbrella she'd purchased locally to protect her head from the rain, as she could not perform her function for the team from within the confines of headgear.

"Left or right?"

"On the left," said Aeomi, gesturing subtly with the forefinger of the hand in which she held the umbrella. The agent dared not move from her position on the street corner just yet, still determined to blend in with the press of bodies moving around, all heads down and in swathed in rain ponchos.

"Facial rec will be a problem, they've been modified heavily with tattoos and piercings," she commented.

Trask zoomed out somewhat and continued searching, the task all the more difficult because of the weather and the fact that most people in the streets were in rain gear. Aeomi had been on his team for two years now, and Trask had never been as thankful as he was now.

The young woman was from the Grotto world of Himar, a planet so radically changed by industry that the population as a whole developed a number of universal mutations. There were countless stories of modern industrial technologies blending with the various unique environments of planets, moons, and asteroids to create virulent new diseases, horrific mutations, and as rumor had it, even monsters. Most of that was just talk of the tug, stories falling from the mouths of salvage marines trying to drink their nightmares into submission, but in the case of Himar, it was very much the truth.

Aeomi, like most everyone else from that planet, had a sense of smell that rivaled any conventional predator. Most Himar citizens wore masks that dampened their abilities so that they could continue to function as members of society, as such sensory perception was a disadvantage for those working in factories or the service sector, which was most of Grotto life.

Aeomi had been a promising enforcer cadet and swiftly rose through the ranks, finding her way into the bond recovery field and onto Trask's team. Without her, this rain would have made the recovery mission much more time-consuming. Like a bloodhound, she was able to lock her mind on the scent of the target and pick them out of a crowd, which was useful considering the tight confines of starships, stations, and urban environments.

Plenty of bond skippers attempted to change their appearance, even going so far as to undergo surgery, but since most skippers were doing so in their position as a result of poverty, such procedures were always black market and often rather cheap.

In an environment where the sun rarely shone through the horrific amounts of polluted cloud cover, the result of unregulated mordite extraction procedures in such massive quantities in such a short amount of time, Aeomi was the perfect hunter. From his position atop the building, he would have had trouble finding them on his own, much less calling out commands to his two agents on the ground.

Lovat, good as he was in a gunfight, was not the best at making clean idents of the targets. Aeomi was key here, and she was making good on that responsibility.

Though he was glad to have her, Trask was still upset about losing his quarry aboard the Yin transit station. As his eyes finally came to rest on a pair of individuals, wearing the same bland ponchos as everyone else, he noticed the brightly colored spiral tattoos on their faces, the polished spikes jutting from their labrets, and the barbells embedded across the ridges of their noses.

Trask had tracked the Chiodo brothers to Yin station, a transit hub for long haulers moving cargo in and out of Grotto space. It was the perfect jump point for someone looking to escape Grotto space for the relative obscurity of the universe at large.

"Lovat, they're closing on your position, walking in tandem, lots of gang furniture," said Trask as he carefully stood from his position on the edge of the building and clipped his repelling harness to the safety line he'd already secured.

"Follow them but don't engage till I give the order, you know how it went down on Yin. These guys are ready to kill, but we still have to make it public enough to meet minimum recovery standards."

"Yes, Boss," growled Lovat, his trademark mirth now gone and replaced by the edge that had seen him through his stint as a warden for the Grotto penal system before joining the bond recovery unit. "Aeomi I'll be back and to the left."

As Aeomi voiced her acknowledgment, Trask braced his feet against the edge of the building and then leaped backward, using his hands to feed line through the rappel clip for a few seconds before his momentum carried him into the wall of the building. He pushed off once more and this time let the line out further, which made his landing a hard one but reduced his descent time by several precious seconds. He could already tell that he was going to need to pop a few more of his med tabs the moment this recovery was over, but these days that had become something of the norm. He had been at this a while, and though his own life bond was paid off, he still had an adult daughter with special needs and her own life bond, so there was no rest to be had for him.

The recovery agent disconnected his clip and drew his poncho's hood over his head. He knew that if the gangers turned they'd see his helmet, there was no hiding that, which was why Lovat and Aeomi were using comm beads and going rig free. The Chiodo brothers had proven themselves to be tough customers, who for all their righteous proselytizing had turned on the people of Grotto rather quickly when faced with a prison sentence.

Trask moved through the crowd, doing his best not to draw too much attention to himself, though with the helmet that was difficult. Thankfully his hunch was right about this place, and like most other depressed urban environments, people just minded their own business, even if it appeared that something interesting or deadly was going down around them. Folks would duck for cover if shooting started, but beyond that, everyone was too busy with the struggle for basic survival to bother caring what was going on.

Which was why when the bond recovery agents did finally engage the Chiodo brothers, it was part of their job to make it something of a spectacle, to remind the citizens of Grotto what awaited them if they attempted to skip on their debts. Doing so without dying in the process took a certain amount of finesse.

Trask used his head's up display to place a visual tag on Aeomi once he caught sight of her umbrella, and then on Lovat when he saw him moving through the crowd, the tall man standing easily a head above most of the populace. His agents were following the brothers on either side of the street, giving Trask the middle, which he skirted just to the right in order to stay out of the path of the occasional vehicles that trundled past.

He watched as the brothers stopped at one of the former luxury vehicles turned storefront and purchased what appeared to be a hot gruel or soup of some kind. Aeomi and Lovat hung back, and Trask moved slowly into the shadows of an awning near the mouth of an alley. He strongly considered attempting to take them here, and normally he would have, had the prey not been the Chiodo brothers.

In his experience, most bond skippers were desperate people fleeing debtors prison, and generally not all that skilled in living life on the run. Grotto corporate life was so regimented and overbearing that the average citizen did not know how to hide, or how to stay in motion without being prompted, much less do so without leaving some kind of trail for agents like him to follow. Factory workers, line laborers, and service people had little in the way of functional experience of life outside of their corporate bubble, and so were generally not difficult to hunt down.

In fact, most bond skippers never made it out of their home system before enforcers scooped them up. It was only those that made it out of that first level of population containment that triggered the transfer of responsibility and jurisdiction from the local enforcers to bond recovery agents. The skippers who made it onto the list of agents like Trask were usually the beneficiaries of overcrowding, bureaucracy, and neglect, and only slipped through the enforcer's nets thanks to something like luck as opposed to any sort of skill. Even so, in the vast corporate society of Grotto, there were many billions of people, and even the tiniest of percentages yielded enough bodies on the run to keep Trask busy for the last twenty years, and his team was one of only several score.

There were dramatically fewer skippers now that the Reaper strike had triggered a reduction in the life bond, but it was a gradual change that would be implemented over decades, and plenty of people facing prison sentences today were still choosing to make a run for it.

Skippers like the Chiodo brothers were rare, though because of the sheer volume of skippers, Trask had dealt with a few 'hard targets' like these men in the past.

The brothers were former union bosses from Trigag Prime, a hellish forge world that supplied a significant percentage of Grotto's heavy equipment machine parts.

In a corporate empire as vast as Grotto, the work stoppage would not have generally been felt so swiftly, that is, until the authorities were forced to take note of the fact that without these critical parts there would be a corporate-wide issue. The union movement on Trigag came to a halt over the course of a single night, and Trask knew from experience that the enforcers had dealt with the union leaders quietly and with extreme prejudice. The Chiodo brothers, however, had managed to escape from the Trigag system, and their case made its way to Jared Trask.

"This is a good place, Boss, nice and public, but not too crowded," observed Lovat from his position across the street, the tall man working to remain part of the scenery by using some of his stash of local chits to purchase two power cells from a street vendor offering refurbished models.

"The food stall forces Aeomi to come around it, and is possible cover, not to mention a potential hostage," responded Trask, keeping his head down and turned away slightly to avoid the brothers taking notice of his helmet.

"These guys didn't hesitate to shoot their way off Yin station, and killed three Grotto citizens in the process, even if two of those were corsec who had assumed the risk when they signed up. We'll hit them once they're on full open ground again."

The brothers were excellent rabble rousers when it came to whipping the workers into a union frenzy, yet abandoned the movement one step ahead of the enforcers. They'd murdered a dock staffer for his ident keys and had disappeared into the black. That was years ago, back during the height of the Ellisian trade war, and it was only a few months ago that the old ident key popped up on Yin station. Even for a case as cold as theirs, it was not the way of Grotto to allow a debt to go uncollected, and the agents were activated. Trask had tracked them there, learned quickly that they'd been working and living as long haulers.

Nobody could hide forever, finally, they slipped up, made a mistake like swiping the wrong ident key while in a rush to board, that's when Trask and his recovery agents showed up to make an example of them.

The brothers finished their food, and instead of paying for it, could be seen revealing the pistols they carried on their hips to the shopkeeper. The man in the stall swiftly dumped a handful of chits on the counter, and Trask could see that he was visibly scared.

These men had likely joined one of the local gangs, which Trask had to admit was a decent cover and were making a life for themselves as thugs. Perhaps not the life the brothers had imagined for themselves back on Trigag Prime, though anything was a preferable alternative to the gulags of the Grotto penal system. Trask hoped they had made the most of freedom while they had it.

"Listen up, people," said Trask, keying commands into his raptor drone, moving in response to the brothers turning with their newly acquired chits and walking further down the street in the general direction of the derelict starport.

"Confirmation that they are armed, and with all that gang furniture it's possible that other members of their organization will respond. We create the spectacle as always, but we need to crunch our extraction time. I have the Raptor One inbound. Aeomi, keep Raptor Two on the surround."

"What about a sanctioned kill window?" asked Lovat as he stuffed the power cells into his pocket and kept pace with the brothers. "I know Grotto loses the meat, but the public still gets a show."

"Negative, Lovat," said Trask while he marched into the middle of the street, slipping his arms inside the slits of his poncho to prime the force shotgun slung over his chest armor, "Incapacitate setting only. We haven't had to retire anyone for a year now and I want it to stay that way. The bond commission plus hazard bonus on these two is more than we'd bank in six recoveries."

"I have plans for that money, Paul," snapped Aeomi as she skirted around the stall and sped up to close in on the brothers, slipping her force pistol from its holster, "Don't blow it for us just because you want revenge."

"These guys are bound for a penal legion, I guess that can be enough," grumbled Lovat as he relented, just like Trask knew he would the moment Aeomi gave voice to her dissent. "Give the word Boss and let's get paid."

The trio followed the brothers for another thirty seconds, just enough to move a modest distance from the food stall. Trask took note of the crowd, and though it had thinned somewhat since they'd started shadowing the brothers, there were easily several dozen individuals in the area.

Determining when and where to take recovery action was a balancing act between a public display of Grotto's power and tactical effectiveness. Trask would have preferred at least five or six more witnesses, though he was not willing to let the brothers get any further. He could see that the tightly packed, makeshift, hab-stack community ahead would give way soon to empty roads and jagged rock terrain.

"Initiating recovery, time now," stated Trask as he pulled his hood back away from his helmet, revealing himself to the crowd while using his voice to activate the recording functions on both their comms channel and his helmet's ocular hardware.

The helmet Trask wore was a recon model that most of the hereditary soldiers for the elite houses used, though it had been heavily modified for recovery duty. In place of the solid armored visor used by stormtroopers, the recovery agent leader was protected by an iridescent plate of plexiglass that had inlaid screens and circuitry. Not only did Trask have access to a number of tracking and communications tools, but the baleful orange glow that the visor now emitted was something of the hallmark of bond recovery agents.

Trask dramatically threw off his poncho to reveal his fully armored self and pressed down on a button on his wrist that activated a series of iridescent lighting strands laid into the edges of his armor, so that parts of him there glowed as well.

Trask keyed his voice caster and started the show.

"Citizens Uri and Martin Chiodo! You are bound by law to stand down!" Trask bellowed through his caster, the device making his voice so loud that the sound of it cut through the patter of the rain and sloppy trudge of boots and wheels through mud, his words were punctuated by the sight of his weapon's wicked muzzle being leveled at the two gangers. "Hands where I can see them, skippers!"

If the booming voice wasn't enough to attract the full attention of everyone in the area, the sight of a man wielding a shotgun and wearing a suit of glowing combat armor certainly was. Most of the Grotto population lived their entire lives without ever seeing a bond recovery agent in the flesh.

In a corporation of hundreds of settled words and billions of people, the ninety or so agents in the field were in an extreme minority. However, when the agents revealed themselves, their armor, weapons, and tactics were intentionally designed to serve as displays of corporate power.

As he peered down the iron sights of his force shotgun, the agent considered how intimidating it must appear in this moment, to see such a thing in the midst of an already dark and depressing place as this. Trask knew that more than anything, he was an instrument of fear, but he had just as many bills to pay as the next person. It was like the Reapers were always saying, this is the job, and Trask did not back down from that harsh reality.

Unfortunately, neither did the Chiodo brothers, who went for their guns the instant Trask revealed himself in the middle of the street.

Uri bolted to the left, not even bothering to turn around, his mind already filled with the image of a glowing bond agent closing in on him.

Trask squeezed the trigger of his weapon as he swung it to track the fugitive, sending a blast of chambered energy from the barrel. The force shotgun was a potent weapon, though Trask had intentionally engaged his targets from just inside its effective range, and the moving field of concussive energy widened as it plowed through the rain towards its target.

Like a standard shotgun, the force weapon was meant for close quarters use in order to take full advantage of its potency and accuracy. Trask had done this many times and was aware that by using the weapon at distance it would cause more visual chaos than it would physical harm.

The field caught Uri's right shoulder and part of his back spinning him around from the impact and depositing him haphazardly into the muddy street.

At the same time, Lovat cast off his own poncho, and though he only wore the modest headgear of a standard agent, his armor glowed with the same fierce light as the Boss. The tall man exploded from the crowd, shoving past two onlookers, and sending them sprawling to the wet ground. His force pistol was out and leveled at Uri as he approached the fallen ganger.

"Uri Chiodo you are bound by law to stand down!" shouted Lovat, his voice nearly lost in the splatter of the rain, but loud enough that Uri's head turned towards him.

Gunfire ripped through the street as Martin Chiodo, his nerves hard as steel, quick-drew his pistol, ignoring the oncoming threat of Agent Trask and going for Aeomi.

The young woman had not yet revealed herself, though the look in Martin's eyes was filled with recognition. He must have made Aeomi back on the street corner somehow, or at least noticed her and then done the math when he saw her face in the crowd after Trask initiated the recovery action. While Lovat and Trask were known to the brothers, Aeomi had been in the guard shack monitoring security feeds when the brothers gunned down officers on board the Yin.

Martin was fast on the iron. In the blink of an eye, he'd cleared the leather of his holster and squeezed the trigger. His weapon was a small caliber machine pistol, with what looked to Trask to be an extended magazine that held at least thirty additional rounds. Even as Trask worked the pump of his shotgun and continued marching forward, Martin's pistol spewed a hurricane of rounds in Aeomi's direction.

Aeomi was still among the crowd when Martin drew on her. She was able to push one woman passerby out of harm's way, but two others paid the price for being near her.

Bullets tore into a man and a woman who had been walking past Aeomi but had stopped to stare once Trask initiated recovery. Of the four people who had once occupied that side of the street, one hit the muddy ground, thanks to Aeomi, two collapsed in a bloody heap, and the agent herself was knocked back into the wall of a building.

The small caliber rounds were unable to penetrate her armor at the modest range, though enough of them pounded into her that Aeomi passed out from the multiple impacts. Her back slammed against the wall, her head snapped back to crack against the hard surface, and then her knees buckled. More bullets chewed into the empty space where her unarmored head had been a split second before Martin cursed as he fought the kicking recoil of his powerful, but difficult to control weapon.

"Thieving scum!" shouted Trask. He leveled his weapon at Martin as the ganger turned his weapon toward Trask.

Trask was dimly aware of more rounds passing into the crowd behind him, as the ganger made it perfectly clear he cared little for the collateral damage he caused.

The agent ignored the pain in his leg and side as a few rounds struck home, each failing to penetrate despite sending damaging shockwaves through Trask's body. The agent squeezed the trigger of his force shotgun. Now that he was closer, the energy field discharge was still somewhat compact when it reached Martin.

The blast displaced the falling rain as it moved. When it hit Martin, the force of it sent the water beading on his poncho hurling in all directions. The ganger's body was picked up off his feet by the discharge and hurled several meters away, landing in a tangle of limbs as he slid through the mud and debris of the street.

Trask already could tell that he'd broken several of the man's ribs, and there was a risk that some irreparable internal organ damage had occurred. Normally he'd have stood his ground, not approached any further, and taken the man down with several lesser potent shots, to make it a show for the onlookers. That was before the quarry had produced the machine pistol, which was a significant step up from the 3D printed homemade guns the brothers had used to fight their way off Yin.

Lovat's attention strayed from Uri for only the briefest of moments when Martin cut loose with the machine pistol, the sigh of Aeomi going down causing his heart to leap into his chest.

Fraternization between co-workers was frowned upon by Grotto corporation in general, though Trask was too much of a hardened veteran to care so long as the pair did their job.

Lovat couldn't help crying out as he saw Aeomi's body hit the ground, the rain and splatters of blood from the people around her making it impossible for him to tell if she'd been wounded or not. That was all the opportunity that Uri needed to roll onto his back and produce his own pistol.

The distinct sound of the heavy revolver's hammer being pulled back snapped Lovat back into focus. The agent twisted his torso to the side and away from Uri, extending his force pistol at the prone ganger.

Uri's revolver was a thud gun, high mass low-velocity rounds meant to maximize knock down power and mitigate penetration. They were designed for shipboard combat, used mostly by space pirates that couldn't get their hands on high-end tech, and were tremendously effective at killing unarmored humans.

Thankfully, for Lovat, he was outfitted with the best body armor Grotto had available, outside of the armor used by the hereditary stormtroopers, and the thud round only knocked him onto his back instead of killing him. Lovat's weapon discharged kicking up a gout of mud as it struck Uri in the leg, propelling the man's prone body across the ground nearly a meter.

Trask racked the slide of his shotgun and turned it on Uri. Before he could fire, the ganger used his off hand to point and fire a phos-flare at the oncoming agent. Trask's discharge went wide and put a huge dent in the metal of a shipping container building just above Uri's position as the agent hurled himself to the ground. The deadly white phosphorous flare round streaked past Trask and bit into the wall of a building on the opposite side of the street. No sooner had it done so the flare's fire slagged a portion of the building easily the size of a transit vehicle.

Trask was furious as he scrambled to his feet and pumped his weapon again. These men were bond skippers, former factory workers, and long haulers, and yet they were fighting like devils. Either someone at Recovery command failed to properly assign the threat level, or he and his team had the bad luck of engaging two men whose talents were blossoming only now that they were out in the larger world. He had encountered such a thing only once before, where a Grotto man who had once been a line cook in one of the great factory cafeterias had skipped his bond and ended up becoming a rather dangerous and disturbingly effective anti-corporate terrorist. Trask had been in his first year as an agent when that happened, and his mentor had died in the fight to bring Metis Anders to heel.

Trask caught a glimpse of Uri dosing himself with a hypo and clambering to his feet.

Trask had only risen to a crouch but managed to fire his force shotgun once more. Uri took the full force of it to the chest. The distance to target had caused the discharge to double in size and lose half its potency, but it was still sufficient to send the ganger over an intersection and into a far wall.

Trask stood and chambered another charge but was quickly forced into cover behind the rusted out ruin of a stripped vehicle as Uri started firing his pistol.

The ganger laid down suppressing fire with the thudder as he ran backward, exchanging fire with Lovat, who had managed to get to his feet and take up position beside a building on the opposite end of the street. Uri was somewhat exposed at the intersection, and the ganger appeared to realize this.

Lovat's jaw dropped as he watched the big man sprint down the street, shoving his way through fleeing onlookers as if they were mere children. Uri was a walking slab of muscle, but even someone that tough could not withstand the kind of force blast that Trask had hit him with.

"How in the verse is that man standing?" rasped Lovat over the recovery channel, his breath ragged from the impact of the thudder, before firing several times into the alley. The agent's force pistol had a better range than the shotgun, though Uri's bracketing fire was making it too risky for Lovat to patiently line up a shot.

"Hit himself with a hypo," growled Trask as he temporarily ignored Uri and keyed in commands for the raptor drone to scoop up Martin's unconscious form. "With all that pirate tech he's carrying it's likely the gang he belongs to has access to other tricks of the trade."

"Combat drugs?" asked Lovat as he attempted to line up a shot only to be forced back as a thud round tore out some of the cement where his face had just been.

"Anti-grav boosters most likely, gives your muscles a serious infusion that keeps them from atrophying," answered Trask as he watched the raptor drone descend from the rainy, gray sky, prompting him to get back to his feet and heft his shotgun. "If used planetside it makes you one tough customer for about ten minutes, but the hangover will put you out for a week easy. I'm moving around, let's flank this bastard."

As the agents prepared to give chase, Raptor One streaked down and landed right over Martin Chiodo's prone form. The drone resembled a bird, hence the name, in that it had fixed wings and an oblong body, though in place of a head it had a sensor array, and where its talons might have been there was a human-sized stasis cage.

When the drone landed it scooped up the ganger's body with the cage, the metal articulating around him as though it was a net thanks to the multitudes of magnetized ball bearings serving as joints, then stiffening again once the body was secured. Compared to most other corporations the technological sophistication of Grotto Corporation was sub-standard, being much less complex even if it was considerably more rugged. Grotto placed a high value on its human capital and factored the labor of the bonded population into almost every aspect of its system. The exception, however, was Bond Recovery. Trask and teams like his were equipped similar to authority operatives in other corporations. The shock and awe of tech such as Raptor One and the forceguns were part of the show meant to keep the population in line.

The sound of an engine revving cut through their conversation, and suddenly a blinding light shone from the alleyway. A moment later the ganger exploded from the side street astride a solo-cycle. The two-wheeled single rider vehicle was equipped with all-terrain tires, and it kicked up mud in torrents as the ganger roared down the side street and turned sharply in the direction of the decommissioned starport. Trask and Lovat looked after him and saw the body of a young man in the street, his throat blown out by what was likely a thud round at point-blank range.

"Raptor Two, inbound!" came Aeomi's voice suddenly, and as the two men turned they saw the young woman soaring through the street, her body several meters above the ground.

Shock and awe, indeed, though Trask as he sucked in his breath. Enforcers or salvage marines certainly weren't going to pull this kind of stunt.

Aeomi had discarded her poncho and had secured her rappel harness to the articulated cage beneath Raptor Two's belly. She was controlling the drone from her wrist pad in the same way Trask had, only the boss agent had never thought to employ the drone in such a way. Trask was a planner, a patient man who did things by the book.

Aeomi zipped past the two men, her pistol in one hand laid over her forearm so that she could not only control the drone but shoot when the time came. This was not by the book, though as she streaked through the rain after the solo-cycle, the boss agent had to admit this op hadn't really gone by the book anyway.

Trask blinked away his shock and started sprinting down the street, as Lovat paused and watched Aeomi chase Uri towards the starport.

"Now that is a bond recovery agent," he whistled, the admiration in his eyes glinting brightly. He rushed to join Trask as the older agent followed on foot. If they pushed their bodies to the limit they might be exhausted when they arrived, but at least Aeomi wouldn't be on her own against Uri for long. Lovat had known bad men in his days as a warden, and though these were supposed to be just factory workers and union malcontents, it appeared that the Chiodo brothers had embraced the ganger life rather profoundly.

The rain stung Aeomi's eyes as she sped through the downpour in pursuit of the solo-cycle, and she was suddenly rather thankful for the awkward folding visors that came standard as part of the agent kit. They also glowed orange, which made her something of a target, but she could see on the faces of the people she passed that witnessing a bond recovery agent screaming through the storm, fangs out, attached to a drone, was making quite the impression. Aeomi was grimly amused at the likelihood of a sharp decrease in attempted skips from this miserable planet after tonight's display of corporate reach and power.

In her experience, despite being only a year in, there were mostly two kinds of skippers. The average Grotto citizen who failed to stay current on their debts and were easily picked up and processed into work camps or penal colonies. They were either rehabilitated or spent their lives repaying those debts with hard labor or military service.

In the core worlds, skippers were usually people who were a little savvier than most, with some resources and at least a modicum of skill just to get past the enforcer screen. They could be dangerous in their own way, but cunning was their primary tool in evading the recovery agents.

Those that came from broken and discarded places like Drill Post 47 were the other sort of skipper, and they were usually a bit more dangerous. Places like this were rough already, and most people out here were living day to day, staying one payment ahead of incarceration. Those that couldn't, who red lined their bond, usually just disappeared into the thriving black market world instead of making the attempt to skip the world.

Enforcers in places like this could be bribed to look the other way more affordably than rehabilitating their debts, so Aeomi had no doubts that upwards of ten percent of the population were red lined and doing their best to hide it. The problem really came when people from places like this did skip. They were usually the hardest of the bunch, most of them criminals of one sort or another, and it took a deadly blend of desperation and skill for someone to skip from here. They were less likely to attempt a cunning evasion like skippers from the core worlds, much more likely for such folk to shoot their way to freedom. When a bond recovery agent got retired, it was usually on the hunt for someone from a place like Drill Post 47.

Drill Post 47 was no different from any other Grotto community gone bust. If seeing the spectacle of bond recovery agents dropping the cage on these brothers prevented even one skipper from making the jump, that seemed to Aeomi like a win. People who dove into the black market world, at least, were still participating in the Grotto economy, even if in a radically illegal way. They might not be paying on their bond, but they were still consuming and still producing, and the Bottom Line was fed its due.

That was the former enforcer in her talking. Aeomi smiled as she flexed her fingers on the handle of her force pistol. Pragmatism was one of the chief virtues of being a citizen of Grotto, even more so as one of the authority figures responsible for maintaining society.

Aeomi's emotions flared as she streaked over the muddy road, freshly ground up by the passage of the solo-cycle. If the people of Himar could find a way to achieve some modicum of identity and prosperity within the Grotto system, then so could the workers on Trigag. When people lashed out at the system, by avoiding work assignment, stealing from others, harming citizens, or dishonoring their debts, they were making a mockery of the Grotto people who stayed loyal and just did their jobs. These Chiodo brothers had stained it with their unionism, not to mention taken the lives of several loyal citizens. Once an enforcer always an enforcer her drill instructor had said, and Aeomi sucked in a lungful of caustic air to clear her head, capturing Uri's stale scent and focusing her mind. She was closing in on Uri and it was time to consider the task at hand.

"Range achieved," reported Aeomi over the recovery channel as she lined up her pistol and let out her breath slowly, doing her best to compensate for the movement of the raptor and the downpour. "Engaging."

Aeomi squeezed the trigger of her force pistol and sent an energy discharge roaring towards her target, the charge burrowing a hole through the rain as it went. She cursed when the charge splattered into the mud right next to the solo-cycle, doing little more than covering Uri in a fresh coat of filth.

The unionist-turned-ganger glanced behind him, and for an instant, their eyes locked. Aeomi could see his pupils widen at the sight of the agent bearing down on him with a raptor drone. She was happy that at she was just as much of an unexpectedly difficult opponent as Uri had turned out to be. She fired again, hoping to catch him off guard, but the ganger was swift to react and jerked his cycle to the right just in time to narrowly avoid another charge.

The agent continued to fire, though keeping a steady aim was proving extremely difficult as she was also having to pilot the drone in response to the solo-cycle. Uri pushed max throttle and the solo-cycle careened down the muddy road, the abandoned starport now looming closer. Aeomi fired once more, managing only to cover Uri and his cycle in mud yet again. The two of them rushed through the night. Aeomi was able to make out a number of barrel fires and lanterns illuminating the inside of the starport. No sooner had she done so than a shot rang out, the report booming over the storm.

Raptor Two shuddered from the impact and immediately lost altitude. Aeomi's next shot went wide, missing Uri completely and slamming into the metal of the nearest support pylon of the starport. The agent's feet were dragged painfully through the mud before she was able to gather them under her and kick off, hoping the boost would help the drone recover. She frantically hit the controls and veered the drone away from the broad face of the starport, hoping that she'd guessed correctly that the sniper was somewhere on that side, as it had a better vantage over the muddy no man's land that separated the city sprawl from the starport.

Out of the corner of her eye, as she struggled to right the drone in spite of the cascading damage alerts that filled her earpiece and flashed on her wrist controls, the agent saw Uri pull his cycle up short and turn to pursue her. Another shot struck the drone, this time from a different weapon. The report was lighter in tone than the first and the impact was less potent as well, though the damaged drone did not have much left to give. Aeomi bought herself a few seconds by rapidly firing several more shots at Uri, forcing the ganger to drive his cycle through one of the massive cargo doors that led into the starport itself.

The agent swiftly adjusted the limping drone's course, and followed the cycle into the starport; the last thing she wanted was to be on foot out in the open. She thought of Trask and Lovat running after her without cover, and knew she had to find a way to occupy the shooters and pursue Uri. The enforcer turned agent cursed at herself for the reckless bravado of her pursuit, she was a bond recovery agent not some elite mercenary from Merchants Militant and had no business assaulting a hardened position. Well, you're in it now, Aeomi, she laughed grimly at herself, might as well just grit your teeth and do the job.

"Unknown shooters in the starport, be advised," snapped Aeomi as she piloted the drone through the cargo doors, "Raptor Two is down, continuing pursuit on foot."

"Disengage, Aeomi! That's an order!" boomed Trask in her earpiece, his breath labored, likely from the dash out of the city and towards the starport. "If he gets dug in with his gang we back off and get a raid team from the Spire."

"I'm over-committed, Boss," said Aeomi as she scanned the interior of the cargo hangar a few seconds before using her controls to slow the drone, only to find it not responding. "Oh, great."

Aeomi looked up and saw Uri driving his solo-cycle up a wide flight of stairs, the man not caring how badly he was damaging the building or the cycle's undercarriage. The agent took a deep breath and grasped the quick release on her rappel harness. An instant later she pulled it, and the drone roared over her head as she fell to the ground. She'd been going at speed, and though Aeomi had anticipated a tough landing, visualizing it and doing it were quite different.

The agent managed to land on her feet and tuck into a roll to slow her momentum, though after the first rotation she lost control and her careful roll became a painful tumble through the debris-laden cargo hangar. At last, she smacked into a stack of empty crates, knocking a few over as her body finally came to rest. Her cheek was cut from either broken glass or a sharp piece of concrete, and her head felt as if she'd taken a bump or two, but the combat armor had protected her from the worst of it.

The agent scrambled to her feet and looked up just as Raptor Two crashed into the cross beams that propped up the second floor. The already badly damaged drone fell in a smoking heap, smashing into the ground and breaking into several pieces. Before she had a moment to consider the drone's fate, gunshots sounded from above, and as no bullets cut through the air to meet her she could only assume that they were shooting at Trask and Lovat.

"Contact high and right!" came Lovat's voice, and though Aeomi was happy to hear him, she was furious that he'd pressed onwards to reach her. For a warden, the man was hopelessly romantic, and unless Trask ordered him to continue the pursuit, his sentiments were going to get him penalized by the after action review board. Not that her overly ambitious move with the drone had been any better, especially now that it lay shattered on the cargo hangar floor.

"I see them," said Trask, and though he said more, Aeomi tuned him out immediately when she saw Uri, having now abandoned the solo-cycle at the top of the stairs, running up a catwalk to the third floor.

The agent sprinted after him, taking the stairs two at a time, pumping her legs as fast and hard as they would go to close the distance between them. She cleared the first set of stairs and almost considered taking the solo-cycle, though she could see once they reached the top why Uri had abandoned it. In his haste, the man hadn't cut the turn sharp enough, and the entire front of the cycle had crunched itself into the base of a display kiosk.

Aeomi sprinted across the terminal as she cranked the output of her force pistol to maximum, vaulting a toppled over a brace of passenger chairs, and took a hasty shot at the base of the catwalk Uri had gone up.

The first hit shook the entire catwalk as it dislodged the base of it from the support screws set into the wall. Aeomi caught sight of Uri as the catwalk started to come down, and she turned and ran the opposite direction she'd been heading, now following the man above her. She fired several more times, each shot blasting apart the thin metal cables that held the catwalk in place. Their tensile strength was tremendous, but the sheer force of the energy discharge unraveled the tightly coiled wires so swiftly and profoundly that they appeared to simply burst apart.

Aeomi reloaded as she ran, then fired again, destroying the catwalk section by section, causing the large metal pieces to fall to the floor in waves behind her. Uri was only one segment ahead of her, and Aeomi raised her pistol. She squeezed the trigger and sent a tightly focused discharge plowing through the cable holding the segment in place.

Uri leaped from the falling segment and thanks to his anti-grav injection his muscles were boosted just enough to help him clear the gap. The ganger's fingers strained as his grip tightened on the ragged metal, the broken pieces biting into his hands when his considerable weight pushed his palms against the edge.

Still determined to make good his escape, Uri flexed his shoulders and began to lift himself up, his biceps bulging from the effort.

"Just give it up already!" shouted Aeomi in frustration as she reloaded again, slotting her last charge pack into the nearly overheated weapon while she kept running towards him.

"Nobody owns me, debt collector!" growled Uri as he worked hard to pull himself up over the edge. "Live free or die."

Aeomi was about to make a clever retort, to needle him about his unionist slogan despite him having abandoned his worker comrades at the first sign of trouble, but she never got the chance. As the agent toggled down the potency of her weapon's output and raised the pistol to take the shot, something moved out of the corner of her eye. In a split second the agent realized it was a person, perhaps one of the shooters, and attempted to sweep her pistol around to defend herself. Before she could, the attacker bashed a homemade weapon into her shoulder.

It was a ganger, that much she could see from the man's spiral tattoos in the brief moment in between seeing him and the impact of his wicked tool. The force of the blow would have been enough to spin her around and take her off her feet, but because of the incredibly sharp spike affixed to the two-handed bludgeon, it turned out much worse. The ganger's stroke put Aeomi on her knees, though he pushed forward, using the spike to drag her across the floor a few feet so that he could drive her head into another display kiosk. The agent stopped moving and wasn't aware of how painful it was when the ganger unceremoniously ripped the spike out of the hole he'd made in her armor and flesh.

Everything was dark, but at least Aeomi knew who she was, and that was a start. The feeling came back in waves as her body woke up around her sense of self. After wakefulness came the pain, and horrible as it was, the trauma of it jerked her out of the darkness. The agent's eyes fluttered open, and the first thing she saw was the silhouette of a large armored figure, lines of glowing orange inlaid throughout the armor to make it appear like some kind of unearthly apparition. Her eyes sharpened slightly as the being came into focus, though when Trask spoke she barely heard it, as the pain of the gaping hole in her shoulder washed over her senses.

"He's one of us now debt collector," snarled the ganger who had so savagely wounded Aeomi, while he stood brandishing his bloody weapon only a few paces from where she struggled weakly to sit up and lean her back against the ruined kiosk, "Can't let you walk in here and take him."

"Shed his blood for the spiral, now he's fam Grotto man!" added a brash and skinny youth who looked to Trask like he'd snap in two if he actually fired the massive scattergun he held leveled at Lovat, then added "Post 47!"

The youth's shout was answered by not just the three men engaged in the point-blank standoff with him and Lovat, but several other voices that echoed through the abandoned starport. The recovery agents had found themselves in the very core of the gang's territory, where neither they nor he, could back down.

"I promise, kid, if this goes gunplay, you die," said Lovat, his voice taking on the warden's edge thanks to his former career. The ex-warden held his force pistol at the base of the neck of a quivering and barely conscious Uri. The former union man turned ganger was coming down off the anti-grav booster, his desperate ploy for freedom only getting him this far, and as Trask had guessed the hangover was going to be brutal.

"Not helping, agent," spat Trask over his shoulder, never breaking eye contact with the ganger he had in his own sights. "Lock it up."

In Lovat's other hand was his warden's service pistol, a weapon that the agent refused to deploy without having attached to his hip, smuggled off the penal colony when he took the contract with Bond Recovery. It was against regulations for any bond agent to carry weapons that fired hard rounds, partially because killing their quarry was never the goal, but also to prevent unnecessary civilian casualties. For once, Trask was happy that he'd allowed Lovat to bring it along even if he did really need Lovat to shut his mouth, as it was now pointed at the skinny youth's shirtless chest, the iron sight level with a crude spiral tattoo in the ganger's dirty skin.

Trask himself had cranked his output to max, and his force shotgun hummed with caged power loud enough that the ganger with the sniper rifle pointed Trask's head would be splattered against the concrete wall the moment he made a wrong move. The agent could see all the ways in which this confrontation was probably going to go wrong and bloody, but it was his job to make the collar and get his people home. He saw Aeomi slowly awaken, and her hand inch towards her fallen force pistol. The ganger who'd taken her down was ignoring her, likely believing her dead or unconscious.

"That man is Uri Chiodo, we have an official recovery warrant, and if you can't tell from our armor and weapons, I can show you our badges," said Trask, hoping against hope that he could push through the typical ganger machismo and reach the human being behind all the swagger, find the young man wise beyond his years from life on the streets, and appeal to his sense of self-preservation. "His brother Martin is gone. He dropped three civilians before we took him. Uri, here, shot another man in the streets. That means the enforcers are going to be looking for someone to blame, someone to punish. Let us take in the men who did it and the '47's won't catch any heat. We can all get out of this."

Trask had talked his way out of worse and genuinely did not want this to become any more of a hostile recovery than it already was. The ganger, apparently, had too much riding on the confrontation happening in his own house to back down. As he spoke, Trask could see it, and though he listened to the man, his eyes narrowed on the sniper in front of him, hoping Aeomi and Lovat were ready.

"Frag the enforcers, lawman!" sneered the skinny youth behind Trask, prompting a wicked smile from the man with the spiked bludgeon, who Trask could see thought, he, at least, was going to survive what was coming.

"Your girl came into my house chasing my fam, got what she deserved. After this gonna get a whole lot more," said the lead ganger, his feet shifting underneath him as he subtly adjusted his stance, a movement so slight that only a professional like Trask took note of it. "Besides, the Spire never sends boots down here, they stay behind their wall. '47's are the law, and you're busted old man."

The ganger sprang forward, faster than Trask thought possible, yet the veteran agent could not afford to worry about him just yet. The sniper's rifle was centered on the agent's head, and he had to contend with that. Trask was faster on the trigger than the sniper, though the agent would go to his grave not fully sure whether he squeezed the trigger first or if the ganger leaped at him first. Not that who started it mattered compared to who finished it.

Trask's force shotgun roared as the agent braced himself against the impact, dropping hard to his knees, his armor the only thing that kept his joints from splintering on the hard floor. The maneuver saved him from the sniper's bullet, which sliced through the air just where his head had been and would have cored his skull had it found its mark.

Trask's own energy discharge struck the sniper in the chest. The man's body flew backward, already pulped inside the suit of skin before it splattered against the pylon behind him. The dead man burst apart from the impact and had Trask not seen such carnage twice before he'd have vomited inside his helmet, the way he'd done twice before. He hated to kill, even men and women who deserved it and had truly hoped to collar the brothers without overly harming anyone. The lead ganger had swung his weapon at Trask's head at the same time the sniper fired, though it too swept through empty air.

Trask racked the slide of his shotgun to drive away the thoughts and prepared to spin around to bring his weapon to bear on the rest of the insanely close quarters fight. His vision was filled with the sight of a spiked bludgeon rushing towards him and was impressed at how swiftly the ganger had recovered from his initial attack and reversed his weapon for another strike.

Trask brought his shotgun up just in time to block the blow, though it had been delivered with enough force that the agent knew instantly that the ganger had dosed with the same anti-grav drugs as Uri. The force of the hit slammed the shotgun into Trask's chest, the weapon bearing the majority of the impact so that the spike only bit into the first layer of the agent's armor. The ganger noticed this and followed up his strike with a swift knee to his own weapon, the impact driving the spike through Trask's armor and into his left lung.

That was when the ganger was hurled to the side by a blast of energy, the backwash of it being enough to knock Trask to the ground. The ganger slammed into the railing, and that was all that kept him from falling down to the first floor.

Aeomi's quaking hands lowered her force pistol, and Trask heard it clatter back to the ground, the young woman's strength all but spent. No matter, his weapon was primed, and the veteran agent couldn't help but growl as he unleashed a blast of energy that hit the ganger so hard that it tore him apart, forcing much of him through the gaps in the railing. This time Trask did vomit, but at least he got his faceplate up soon enough to spill his latest meal across the grimy floor.

"Not to rush you, boss, but we've got company on the way," insisted Lovat as he helped Trask to his feet and yanked the spiked bludgeon out of his armor.

Trask took a shallow and pained breath, returned his faceplate to its locked position, and looked out across the starport. He could see the corpse of the skinny ganger, the scattergun laying unfired on the ground next to him. The former warden had been fast on the trigger indeed, and Trask wondered if Lovat had the same questions about who started this bloodbath, them or the gangers.

"Dose Aeomi with stims and get her moving," said Trask as he swiftly injected himself with a dose as he looked about the starport, taking in the sight of more gangers cautiously moving in on their position, "I'll clear us some space and help you with Uri."

Trask stepped out to the railing, intentionally standing on top of the grisly remains of the ganger he'd just obliterated. The agent keyed his voice caster and throttled the volume up to compensate for the wheeze in his voice caused by the injured lung. He made a show of blasting a crater of concrete out of the third-floor ceiling. As the concrete chunk smashed against the floor, he began to speak.

"Post 47! I am Bond Recovery Agent Jared Trask, duly licensed by Grotto Corporation to execute the recovery warrant of Martin and Uri Chiodo. During the course of my duties in pursuit of these fugitives, it has been brought to my attention that the Chiodo brothers have bled on the spiral and are now fam with the '47's. As such you may be operating under the same illusions as your dead comrades," boomed the amplified voice of the bond agent as behind him Lovat worked to get Aeomi up and conscious before moving to bind Uri with mag-clamps and tie his legs up with a thin cable dispensed from a box spool at his belt.

"As an agent on duty, my ID and location are uploaded to the Spire every thirty seconds, as are those of my two subordinates. If we are not allowed to leave this starport unmolested, the full might of the Spire will come down on Post 47. As you know, Grotto prefers you alive as a slave rather than dead as a free man. Stand in my way and enforcers will not only take the '47's, but your children will inherit your debts, and soon follow you into an oblivion of labor and war. Make your choice!"

The pronouncement was met with silence, and Trask dared to hope. The agents struggled down to the bottom floor, and still, no more gangers revealed themselves, much less opposed them. It was slow going, with two wounded agents and a recovery in tow, but they made it out into the open without further incident. Minutes after they left the starport the running lights of an enforcer barge could be seen speeding across the wastes.

"I still can't believe we made it out of there," said Lovat as he shook his head in the spotlight of the descending barge, repeating himself for the third time since they'd made good on their exit. "That voice cast really did a number on them."

"It was only the truth, nothing more and nothing less," sighed Trask as he turned his head to face Lovat. "That's what made it so effective. Nothing inspires more fear than the cold hard truth."

PROSPECTOR PIRATES

The *Rig* shook as it moved through the upper atmosphere of the unexplored planetoid Osi 2216. The ship's geologist, a man who called himself Braeden the Red, had been overjoyed about the readings his scout drones had returned. According to Braeden, there was a significant probability of sizable ink-rock deposits just beneath the crust of the planetoid.

On this distant fringe of mapped space multitudes of worlds had only been given the most cursory of surveys, often simply being named and charted without any surface expeditions. The universe was simply too vast and dangerous for there to be much incentive for cartography ships to undertake any but the most lucrative of expeditions. This was compounded by the fact that most planets held little in the way of valuable resources to extract, much less were capable of sustaining life, so exploration was generally left up to desperate red listers, freelance colonists, pirates on the run, or prospectors such as the *Rig Halo*.

Braeden had observed the planet from a distance, using the *Rig's* long-range scanners to scrutinize its potential. After his initial evaluation the geologist had recommended a closer inspection, and the pilot, Meridian, had brought the ship into the upper atmosphere. Once again, their secondary readings were promising, so the pilot had brought them low enough to launch scout drones. There were three of them, patchwork robots of Braeden's own design, that took soil and rock samples, returning to the geologists onboard lab for evaluation. It was a relatively swift process, one that the crew of the *Rig* had gotten very efficient at executing. In just a few hours, the geologist and his support team, along with the pilot and the ship's crew, could make a final assessment about a planet. While the majority of planets encountered were of no value to the prospecting ship, when they did find one, Braeden had yet to be wrong in his judgment.

Osi 2216 had been no different, though it had not required quite so much from the geologist this time, as one of his drones had been fired upon by someone already on the ground. While the geologist conducted his tests in the lab, Meridian, at the captain's orders, took the ship along the path the drone had taken. They had found who had been doing the shooting. As the ship made a wide arc around the source of the incoming fire, Samuel Hyst stood in his quarters with his wife as he prepared to disembark.

The couple was silent, having known this day would come, though neither had thought it would be so soon. The first prospect had been easy, a swift assessment on an uninhabited asteroid lazily floating through the void.

Samuel had worked with Yanna on the drilling team, his skills as a welder proving rather useful as he used his Reaper's torch to keep the grooves of the drill free from the molten ore that kept locking it up. The Grotto torch was designed to be small and focused, more for cutting than it was for joining, and thanks to his ability to use it for detailed work Samuel was able to keep the drill clean without Yanna having to stop her process. In the end, Samuel's presence had saved an estimated forty hours of labor, which meant that the ink-rock ended up on the exchange desk before a recent price spike had flattened out.

He should have known that it wouldn't be so easy for long, thought Samuel, as he fastened his forearm bracers together. Sura buckled his chest plate to his backplate, deftly sliding the interlocking pieces of each plate together before affixing the locks that would encase her husband in a protective shell.

The Reaper armor had seen better days, he reflected, noticing the multitude of metal patches he'd made after the fight with the Tasca cartel operatives, blending into the various repairs and upgrades the suit had endured during his years of service. He couldn't help laughing as he reminded himself that there never had been better days, to begin with.

"What about any of this has given my husband a reason to laugh?" asked Sura as she came around to face Samuel, and then smiled as she undid and re-fastened one of his hip pieces.

Samuel winced at the mistake, a frustrating reminder that his range of movement was modestly limited thanks to those Tasca bullets embedded in his Augur issued spinal implant.

The hardened metal of the spine grafts had prevented him from dying when the operatives sank rounds into him back on Longstride, though they had slightly damaged some of the articulation. Leaning and bending to his left had become something of a problem, and though it had been months now since he was shot, it had become clear that until he risked discovery and paid a hefty sum to have the bullets removed by an Augur tech specialist he was going to have some mobility issues. Today that meant that his wife, now intimately familiar with the armor, had to double-check his work on that side.

"I was thinking about the patches on the armor, and how it never looked new in the first place," answered Samuel after a moment, nodding in thanks as he accepted the helmet Sura offered him from its wall mount next to their bed and slotted it over his head. "All these years living in this armor, and I never once wondered who wore it before me. What that man's life was like, if he got early retirement or if he managed to get all the way through his service."

Samuel tapped the nameplate on his chest, the word 'Hyst' now burned away, leaving only a black streak through the metal.

"Without the stencil how can you even know it's me in here?" asked Samuel before he shook his head and slung his rifle over his shoulder. "I am getting sentimental in my old age."

"I like that about you," said Sura with a gentle laugh as she rested her arms around his shoulders and raised herself up on her tiptoes to deeply kiss his darkened faceplate, and then pulled back to look where she thought his eyes were. "This is a second skin, that gets the job done and brings Samuel back to me."

"Not always in one piece," said Samuel as Sura stepped back so that the marine could move through their small room towards the door as the starship shook from turbulence.

"You stitch together just fine, marine," observed Sura warmly as her eyes appeared to sparkle, tilting her head ever so slightly to the side even as she turned on the balls of her feet a few degrees, giving her husband a last eyeful of her smooth neckline and the swell of her curves, a promise of what waited for him upon his return. "Good hunting."

The door closed behind Samuel, and he started to take a step down the corridor, before stopping. He turned, and almost opened the door again. The marine lowered his hand and then leaned forward to rest his forehead against the metal of the door. He closed his eyes and fought against the urge to go back inside. After more turbulence shook his eyes open, the marine straightened up and walked down the corridor towards his mission with resolve.

Sura still stood on her side of the door, with her head against the metal, the tears falling from her eyes splashing across her bare feet. Her own mission would be plenty dangerous, and it was not only her husband who was going to get shot at today. Samuel would no doubt be furious with her if they both survived what was coming, but she had known better than to fill him in on the details. She knew the *Rig* in ways that he had yet to learn, and if they were going to make a life here, both of them had to do their part. Sura pulled on her boots, affixed her tactical harness, and pulled her long coat over her shoulders.

Let him have one clean fight, she told herself as she picked up her lever action rifle with one hand and wiped away her tears with the other, before he learns the truth.

"Mind the wheel, Corin, this rover is worth more than you are," growled Narek as the former battle trooper's body was shaken hard against the restraints keeping him in the passenger seat next to the young merc who drove the all-terrain vehicle. "Besides we wouldn't want our war hero to chuck his breakfast before the shooting starts."

Samuel chose not to respond to the trooper's jibe and simply held himself firm in his seat just behind Narek. His own restraints were pulled taut as they kept him in place while the surprisingly nimble vehicle rushed across the rocky terrain.

Despite the trooper's mean-spirited banter, which had been constant since the group of gunmen had gathered in loading deck of the Rig for a short briefing before deployment, he was right about the rover itself. The vehicle rode high on six wheels and three axles, each one operating independently so that the rover could overcome most any terrain. The cab seated the six gunmen comfortably, and the additional plexiglass armor affixed to the titanium roll cage made visibility easy while still yielding some degree of protection from ambush.

Behind Samuel stood Garn, one of the other mercs, with his hands at the ready upon a light machine gun currently affixed to a mount on the top of the roll cage.

The weapon was old, a Fenrir Industries brand urban assault model, discontinued after being used to horrific effect by gun cults during the Torrid Uprising. While the weapon was illegal in nearly every system in corporate space, and ammunition was likely very difficult to come by, Samuel was happy to have it on their side. He'd have preferred Ben Takeda or Harold Marr and their Grotto heavy machine guns at his back, but out here on the ragged edge of civilization, Samuel took what he could get.

The other two mercs in the rover with him, Jayce and Michael, were more like Corin, in that they were mercs of no particularly distinguishing characteristics. Just three men who fell into a life of the gun, wearing patchwork armor and carrying whatever weapon suited them, instead of anything standard issue. Whether they had formal military training or not, they had no doubt proven themselves in the eyes of Narek, who led them in a manner not dissimilar to the long-dead Boss Taggart. They reminded him in a way of how he tended to see the new marines that filled the empty armor of fallen friends. Of all the Reapers who came and went in Tango Platoon over the years, the medic, Holland, and the flame trooper, Gretchen, who was now presumably the mother of Ben's child if she was still alive, were the only ones he could clearly remember. Only those marines with whom he went through basic were crystal clear in his mind, the rest were lost in the churn of war and salvage.

Samuel looked out across the front of the rover and could, at last, see the columns of debris smoke that rose from over the ridge ahead. The wind on the planet was a wicked thing, proving rather strong and unpredictable, and the swirling pillars of dust and rock going from the ground to the sky above dotted the landscape. What made those in front of them different is that these were tinged with black, which Samuel knew was from the ink-rock that was being mercilessly torn from the planet's sub-surface by an as yet unknown mining operation.

Samuel knew nothing about them, other than the modest intel they'd been given at the briefing. Braden's drone captured shots of a relatively small mining operation, one of the pre-fab compounds and drilling rigs that was of the same style, even if smaller, than what the *Rig Halo* would deploy.

There were an estimated twenty human beings present in and around the complex, though with atmospheric conditions being what they were it was difficult to know for sure. It stood to reason that the operation would have a support ship somewhere on the planet, though it had not yet been located. Though it had not been specifically mentioned in the briefing, Samuel thought it likely that Captain Dar intended to use Narek's violent disruption of the mining operation to flush out the support ship. 2216 was an unclaimed world, open to exploitation by anyone with the capacity to take it and hold it. The marine knew as well as anyone that if a major play was discovered, more than a single score for a lucky freelancer, it would only be a matter of time before corporate forces would arrive to fight it out and build a major factory operation. Any independent prospector operation was wise to fill their cargo hold and make a hard burn for the black, whether they were leaving a play behind or not, as there would always be someone coming to contest the claim or seize it outright.

"Two miles from the target, boys," said Narek in his ragged voice, his accent combining with what Samuel presumed to be some old battle wound that gave his voice an almost comical grit. "If they've got snipers or bushwhackers in place we'll be rousing them soon, so keep your heads behind that glass."

According to the briefing the team of gunmen were to make a bold assault on the compound, rushing in and overwhelming the rig staff before any real firefights could break out. There were in fact only six of them moving against a compound with at least twenty hostiles, though most, if not all of them would be non-military. That wasn't to say that they wouldn't be armed, but that unless they had their own mercs on the payroll, these people would be laborers and tech staff, none of whom were likely to put up much of a fight.

"You ready for this, Reaper?" spat Narek as he looked over his shoulder at Samuel, his clear faceplate not yet turned to the icy reflective blue that indicated the Helion lite power armor had been activated. "Hope you didn't lose your edge after spending all those years pulling weeds and growing potatoes."

"Turnips, actually," said Samuel as he flexed his fingers and moved his rifle across his chest into the ready position, "Potatoes are for amateurs."

Garn let out a subdued laugh as he thumbed off the safety of the mounted Fenrir weapon. The other mercs shared the cheap laugh, and Narek's expression darkened. Samuel didn't look away from the man, and they held each other's gaze for a moment. It was hard to let go of old hatreds, and neither man appeared to be doing a good job of it.

Samuel took a deep breath and then inclined his head towards the dark swirling columns of ink-rock debris.

"The dust we're kicking up won't register to them as a threat, given the chaotic landscape. The captain's plan is a good one. Unless they have more sophisticated scanners that can cut through this mess we'll be on top of them before they know we're coming," observed Samuel, making sure to key his voice into the squad channel so that all the mercs could hear him over the roar of the wind and the crunch of rocks under the all-terrain tires of the rover. "That means the drill will be active when we hit them."

"Dammit," grumbled Narek as he activated his Helion armor and turned to face the front of the vehicle. "Captain thinks of every little detail, no way he overlooked the most obvious problem. Bastard is gambling with our lives. Again."

"What's the problem?" asked Corin as he turned the wheel to avoid a large boulder that even the rover wasn't going to be able to move over without being turned on its side.

"If the drill crew is fast enough on the draw they can spike a charge into the chute," answered Garn from his perch behind the rest of the mercs.

"At best it slags the drill and forces us to dig our own chute," said Samuel, "Which cuts deep into our timetable and expenditures, and we will probably miss the positive rate window at the exchange desk. Price could bottom out while we're still trying to extract the juice."

"At worst it's a suicide bomb that takes out the whole compound," said Narek as he cranked the dial on his rifle to prime the Helion hot rounds, the sound of it making Samuel's trigger finger itch with troubled memories. "This is why I said we should never seize an active claim. Better to just defend our own."

"Payout is going to be cherry though," offered Jayce with a wicked smile as he checked the chamber on his auto-pistol and slotted home an extended magazine, his seeming eagerness to get into the fight making

Samuel wonder what sort of merc work the young man had been doing prior to joining the Rig, "They did all the work, we're just making some changes to the staff roster."

Sura's hair whipped about in the harsh winds that cut through the platform's open structure, though with her goggles and the bandana she had pulled up over her mouth the swirling grit did not bother her eyes or hamper her breathing. She stood just behind and to the left of Captain Dar, with Braden standing back and to the right of him, all of them making sure that their hands were kept in plain view and away from their weapons.

The five men standing around them were respectfully doing the same, though she'd noticed right away that all of their sidearms were set loose in their holsters for swift drawing, and the two men with shotguns had left the safeties off before slinging them to the side.

She took in the sight of the platform around her while Captain Dar's strong voice carried over the howling wind. She'd listened to him work his pitch as Braden drove the small ATV to the rendezvous point several miles out, where they'd met up with two of the rival prospector's armed escorts. The men with shotguns had then led them here to the mining compound for a face to face with management. She smiled inwardly at how slick her captain could be when he wanted and admitted to herself that the man could probably sell water to a fish if he wanted to. As it was, the captain was attempting to convince the owners of the rival mining operation to sell him their current haul of ink-rock at a steep discount, saving them the hassle of shipping and saving him the trouble of mining it himself.

"You already have an operation in place, and I respect that. We aren't here to dispute your claim, nor to attempt staking our own anywhere else on this world. We buy your haul and we leave, you keep drilling, and everyone has a chance to get paid sooner," concluded Dar, having made his pitch twice now, this time in person to the executive of the rig, who appeared none too pleased that the captain had gone over his head and communicated directly with his operation's owners. "Your superiors felt that this was a strong enough offer to warrant a tour of your facility and a core sample, hence the presence of my geo-specialist, Mr. Braden here."

"Show me proof of funds or get the hell off my planet," snapped the mining foreman as he pointedly ignored Dar's gesture acknowledging Braden, the man's rough hands and ink soiled coveralls marking his as a working man just as much as management. "That prospecting license gets you a meeting instead of a bullet, that's all you get on good faith. Until I see a positive balance in a registered account there's nothing else to discuss. Ackerman and Jema might own this outfit, but they aren't running it and they never go stationside, so they don't hear what we hear. *Rig Halo* has a clean official record, but the talk is that your positive reputation is starting to get stained with rumors of piracy."

At that moment, Sura was keenly aware of their plan, and the implied accusation dredged up more than a few unsavory memories of past conflicts. During her brief time aboard the *Rig,* she had killed her fair share of men and women, but they were all defensive actions. Claim jumpers or violent squatters, and thus far she'd managed, with help from Dar, to rationalize and justify those deaths. This was a hard universe, she knew that more than most, but the *Rig* and its crew had never, to her knowledge, stooped to piracy. Things were different now, that much she knew, and the line between prospector rivalries and outright piracy had gotten blurred. It wasn't just for Dar and his operation, but for every freelancer out there, licensed or not.

She had been afraid to ask Dar about what had happened since they'd parted ways, knowing that his answers would only complicate things between her and Samuel, as the marine was still adjusting his moral compass to the harsh realities of their new life. Then she thought of the captain's true plan, their real purpose in this meeting, and she was forced to accept that her values were far more flexible than her husband's. Part of it was pragmatism of course, but Sura suspected that she enjoyed the rush of danger more than she was prepared to admit to herself, or to Samuel. She had to fight the urge to rest her hand on the grip of the ganger combo revolver strapped to her hip, allowing it to rest beneath the folds of her long coat for a few moments more.

"Rumors always follow success, and we've had plenty of that. The trade war was hard on everyone, but we've made do without having to cross any lines I can assure you," answered Captain Dar with open hands, before slowly lifting a small datapad from his chest pocket and tapping in an access code. "But I get it. Ackerman is resting comfortably aboard the Etheria, floating in orbit on the other side of the world, while you're here doing the real work and taking the real risks. The money is real, look for yourself."

Captain Dar stepped forward and held out the tablet, which the foreman took and began to read intently. Sura knew from their briefing that to make the deal appear legitimate, Captain Dar had pooled every last scrap of liquid assets from the crew, including the ship's emergency reserve account. In order to appear like real buyers, they had to have the money to make good on the pitch. The foreman's eyes widened slightly as he looked over the account, and Sura could see his shoulders relax slightly. It was a small fortune, and after a steep discount, the *Rig* truly could afford to purchase the existing haul of ink-rock now stored in the compound's silos. The *Rig* could fill its hold to the brim and then bring the ink-rock to market in a matter of days. The mining operation gained in convenience and lowered risk exposure more than what they lost in the discount, and the *Rig* did not have to contest the claim or set up their own operation. That was why the plan was going to work because it was perfectly plausible.

"Well, Captain, it looks like your money is where your mouth is," nodded the foreman, who then spoke into the comm-piece affixed to his chest after nodding at his men, each of them visibly relaxing.

"Meechum, this is Kat, get your boys on the drill to pull a core sample. I'm bringing some guests down, got a buyer and his geo-specialist to sample the juice."

The foreman turned and gestured for the trio to follow him, and while the other individuals on the platform returned to their various jobs, Sura was not surprised that the two men with shotguns fell in behind them.

Braden went after the foreman, walking down the stairwell in the middle of the structure that would take them towards the central drilling platform, with Dar behind him and Sura at the end. The unspoken truth was that if the price of the ink-rock bottomed out while the *Rig* was in transit, then they'd be broke and on the drift, having bet everything on the single run. Sura half-hoped that the captain would change his mind, and that they'd actually go for it. Nobody had to die in that scenario, and no lines would be crossed.

Dar cast a glance at Sura, and she could see that he was strongly considering it, the struggle plain on his face. To anyone else, he'd have simply appeared uncomfortable in the gritty gale of the winds that continued to buffet the structure, but Sura knew the man well and had learned to read the more subtle clues in his demeanor.

The captain was deeply conflicted, and she knew he was on the verge of just pushing ahead with the deal. He had a transmitter that could be keyed, and despite the atmospherics, it was a direct link to Narek's squad. He could call them off at any moment, and the *Rig* could take its chances with the exchange desk.

Sura gave the captain the slightest of nods, and his shoulders visibly relaxed. They'd make the buy. Dar slowly reached for his transmitter, and then a sudden gust of wind forced him to grab the railing to keep himself steady.

As the group began to exit the stairwell onto the drilling platform Dar's transmitter activated, and though Sura could not hear what was said, she knew that there was no going back. Perhaps it had already been too late before the captain changed his mind, or perhaps not, and she wondered if such questions would haunt Dar after this, assuming they survived.

The foreman inclined his head as his own comms rig began filling with traffic. The foreman's eyes snapped up to Dar and then drifted up to the men behind Sura. She half-turned her face and looked over her shoulder just in time to see the two guards putting their hands to their ears in the way that people often did when one ear had a comms piece and the other did not. One of them looked down at her and reached for his shotgun. She shook her head gently, hoping he would stop as her own hand drew the long coat back so that she could go for the revolver.

A single round had impacted against the front windshield of the vehicle, and though it did not penetrate, the crater it made in the glass right in front of Corin's face revealed the skill of the shooter. Corin cranked the wheel instinctively and for a moment the rover veered dangerously hard to the left, though in an instant the merc corrected and the rover plowed forward undeterred. Two more shots pounded into the plexiglass, leaving spiderweb cracks in their wake across the right flank. Samuel hadn't seen where the secondary shots had come from, but as Garn opened up the marine followed his cone of fire to the jagged outcroppings of stone and dirt on their right.

The trees on this world were gnarled and twisted things, snaking horizontally like tentacles instead of growing tall and proud as one might expect. It made Samuel miss Longstride for a tiny moment, with its cloud cover and thick forests covering the rolling hills, untouched by the machinations of industry or agriculture.

Garn's fusillade tore through stone and tree alike, sending up bursts of splinter and rock shard as the weapon belched forth a stunning number of bullets. They were small caliber rounds but packed a significant amount of power, and Garn's ammunition drum contained over two hundred of them. As Samuel kept his eye on the tracer rounds he saw a bloom of red mist appear as Garn's weapon chewed its way across the rocky treeline, and then a second bloom just as the rover sped out of the ambush zone.

"High gear, Corin, and floor it!" ordered Narek as the rover burst out of the valley and began speeding across the half mile of open ground between them and the base of the mining compound.

"Captain, we've been made!" spat Narek into his comm-bead, though the only reason Samuel heard it was that Narek was shouting, the actual traffic going through a different channel which appeared to be just for the merc and the captain. "We're coming in hot so keep your head down!"

"Wait, Dar is in the compound?" asked Samuel as Corin turned the wheel left and then right again so that he could jink out of the way of several boulders and a few of the odd horizontal trees that had managed to force their roots through the hard packed ground in spite of the heavy winds that made the rover buck and pitch.

"Roger, he's working an angle with their management," nodded Narek as the rover drew close enough to the compound that Samuel could see staffers scurrying about the structure, some of them appearing to flee while others looked to be preparing to defend against the oncoming mercs. "Something about minimizing collateral damage. Don't worry, he's got your lady with him, the talk is she's good at watching his back."

Something tugged at Samuel's heart, and he found himself seeing red. The marine rose up in his seat, ready to slam the stock of his rifle into Narek's leering face. The former battle trooper was baiting him, and somewhere in the back of his mind he knew that, but the matter-of-fact way in which the man had spoken halted Samuel. The marine moved back into his seat, under full cover of the armored sides, and not a moment too soon as several shots pinged against the rover.

The man with the shotgun did not stop, and Sura exploded into action, her body already tightly coiled in anticipation. Sura surged upwards, clearing the three steps between her and the man as her combo pistol cleared leather with a speed and precision born from relentless training. The shotgun was swinging towards her, though before the man could get it leveled at her, Sura's left hand slammed, open palmed, into the action of the weapon. Sura used the combined force of her blow and her forward momentum to pin the shotgun against the man's waist, activating the quick-release bayonet affixed to the bottom of her revolver.

The housewife turned freelance prospector had become a gunfighter years ago, though she was still finding new ways to appreciate the wicked particulars of the combo revolver. It had arrived on Samuel's hip when he'd returned from the trade war, and at first, she had thought it was a trophy. It was only later that she discovered its sentimental value and the rugged functionality that made it such a storied prize.

Samuel had been willing to share stories from his time with the Reapers of Baen 6, though the campaign that had scarred him the deepest had been the liquidation of Vorhold. He would speak little of it, though had been willing to share the story of a man named Vol.

The revolver had belonged to the downspire ganger, who had wielded it with a savage grace as he fought alongside Samuel in the bitter darkness. Apparently, after Vol died in the rescue of several marines, Ben Takeda among them, Samuel's leader Wynn Marsters ended up with it. Boss Marsters had carried it for years in the Ellisian trade war, though after the Reaper strike had bequeathed it to Samuel for his journey onto the frontier.

It was crafted for rough use, capable of utilizing nearly any sort .44 caliber ammunition, whether those were the sleekly manufactured cartridges produced by Fenrir Industries or the homemade wildcat rounds that were more common among the destitute and the daring.

The bayonet, which slid across well-oiled rails on the bottom of the weapon's barrel, made it equally devastating as a close quarters weapon.

With his hands wrestling for control of the shotgun, and certainly not anticipating a revolver with a bayonet, the man had only a moment to register what was coming. Sura howled in a mixture of combat fury and disappointment at the sudden, but not unexpected, downturn of events as she drove the blade through the man's neck, the point of the weapon punching through the other side of the man's flesh.

The second guard leveled his shotgun at his comrade's back and paused, still in shock at the manner of the man's unlikely death and seemingly unsure of whether to shoot or not. Sura twisted her wrist to force the angle of her gun sideways instead of upright, and the bayonet tore an even greater wound in the dying man's throat as she did so. Now the barrel was clear of the first guard's body, and Sura fired on the second guard just as he desperately squeezed the trigger of his shotgun.

The combo revolver thundered as it hurled a heavy round through the second guard's chest, the force of it picking him up and throwing him backward against the stairwell. The guard fired a microsecond after Sura, and his aim was spoiled by the impact of the projectile.

The cloud of shot ripped into the right side of the first guard's body, finally ending his life and making his knees buckle. Sura was protected from the blast, though the power of it knocked her off balance and sent her tumbling down the remainder of the stairwell along with the corpse of the man she'd skewered.

Sura's head bounced off the hard edge of one of the last stairs, and her world went black. An instant later her eyes fluttered open and she felt a hand grasping her collar and dragging her by the coat across the metal flooring of the compound. Her vision swam as she looked up, and when it came into focus a moment later she saw that it was Captain Dar pulling her.

The captain was keeping up a high rate of fire, moving his weapon this way and that, giving Sura the impression that he was trying to keep heads down more than he was trying to hit anything, or anyone, in particular. She looked back, over her boots, and saw a body dressed in worker's coveralls sprawled upon the deck, and off in a distance made hazy by the gritty wind that ceaselessly blew across the rig, she saw other people running and returning fire.

Dar let go of her once he'd gotten Sura behind a large stack of drill pipes. As the captain reloaded, Sura gathered herself and shook the last of the cobwebs from her mind. Her head was bleeding, and she could see fresh red dripping down on her neck and onto her shoulder. Head wounds bled profusely, even minor injuries, and so the blood was no indication of how bad it might be. Either way, she'd need attention quickly, though in the heat of a gunfight, time had a way of grinding to a crawl, and for that she was thankful.

Sura realized that she still had the revolver in her hands, and the sight of it reminded her of why they'd come armed in the first place. Surely it was customary and prudent to be armed at all times in necrospace, and nobody would fault them for that, not even at a tense business negotiation, though the real reason was the drill. They had to stop the prospectors from hurling an explosive down the chute.

"They're going for the drill!" shouted Dar as he turned from his firing position and crouched down to reload his own pistol, "Get back in the fight, Kameni!"

The use of her maiden name snapped Sura back to attention, cutting through the haze of her head trauma. Technically speaking, though she went by the name Sura Hyst, she and Samuel had been divorced for years. It had been part of their bid for freedom years ago once, to release she and Orion from any debts Samuel might incur, now that their life bonds were cleared. She and the marine had never formally re-married and had just gone on living their lives as if it had been only a matter of paperwork. Captain Dar called her by her maiden name when he wanted to express his feelings for her, which she knew by now were more genuine and complex than physical desire. He was an honorable man, at least when it came to his crew, and had never pressed the matter beyond the use of Kameni. It was a minor trespass, and one she admitted that she had never objected to or asked him to correct. At that moment the cascade of conflicting emotions brought her to full alertness.

Sura cocked the hammer of her revolver and used her off hand to rotate the cylinder over to one of the flare rounds. She leaned out of cover and fired it at the center of the platform, the round streaking through the swirling dust and slamming into a piece of large machinery. The flare illuminated the platform only marginally, but the multitude of micro-reflections cast by the wind-borne particle storm was enough to elevate the ambient light enough for she and Dar to see their enemy. No sooner had she done that than a prospector sprinted across the platform towards the primary drill mount and gripped tightly in his hands was a rock melter, one of the focused charges often used to start a new drill chute.

Sura's revolver roared as she fired at the running man, though her shot went wide and bit into a pylon, doing little more to the prospector but shower him with sparks. Dar had better luck, and his bullet thudded into the rival prospector's ribs, sending him spiraling and crashing to the deck. The executive who'd called himself Kat leaned out from behind a large metal crate and returned fire with a small pistol he must have had secreted away in his waistband, driving both Dar and Sura back into cover even as one of his guards attempted to work his way close enough to the pair to use his shotgun effectively. Sura realized suddenly that she had not seen Braden since the fight started and wondered if he'd survived thus far.

Which was just as well, as a moment later the real gunfight began, sending everyone on the platform scrambling for safety.

Samuel had known that Sura had learned how to shoot and fight while serving aboard the Rig, and though she did not like to talk much of her time aboard prior to Samuel's arrival, he knew she'd seen her share of violence. Sura was a woman of Grotto, and so she approached life with the same hard pragmatism that everyone else from the corporate society often did.

Samuel, himself, while certainly a man who had struggled and strained against the corporate world and Grotto culture, had that same pragmatic streak. While he had fought in the trenches of distant wars and killed during hostile salvages aboard derelict spacecraft, his estranged wife had been fending off claim jumpers and pirates alongside Captain Dar and the crew of the *Rig Halo*. He should not have been surprised to learn that she was in the thick of danger, though he was furious that Narek, Dar, and Sura herself had kept that truth from him.

She was in there somewhere, and all of a sudden the four platforms that comprised the structure seemed rather vast, whereas moments before the target felt small and manageable. Now it was a labyrinth of stairwells, heavy machinery, and hostiles.

Perhaps she thought the shooting would be over one way or the other before he found out, for surely she could not have been so callous as to not care. Sparing his sensibilities the distraction and worry of his wife in harm's way was more likely, Samuel thought to himself, at once angry with his wife and ingratiated to her for the concern over his own ability to focus upon the task at hand. The universe had always been hard on the Hyst family, and it appeared that today was no different than any other.

"Garn, get these mosquitoes off my back!" growled Narek. The sporadic gunfire coming from the compound increased as the rover drew near, and the gunner nodded as he took aim. "Corin I want you to jump that first barricade, the rover can take it, then we're bounding from there, boys."

"Copy," said Samuel, his voice more steady than he felt, and his word was echoed by the other mercs just before Garn's machine gun roared behind them, drowning out all other sounds.

As the rover neared the compound, Garn's cone of fire washed over the ground floor, and this time the carnage was not hidden by bursts of stone and wood. Men and women in orange jumpsuits scattered as many of them were cut down by the hurricane of small caliber rounds. Sparks flew in showers as the gunner unleashed sustained fire, moving his weapon side to side to hose down a full one hundred and eighty-degree field of fire. The rover was almost to the base of the compound, and in the last seconds before they jumped the barricade Garn angled his weapon up and managed to spray several bursts of deadly projectiles into the second platform.

Corin earned his rate as he gave the rover a burst of power at the last second and clamped down on the brakes of the back two all-terrain tires. The maneuver shot the nose of the rover upwards and the momentum of the vehicle carried it over the prefab railing barricade of the compound. The thin metal of the barricade was meant to keep out dust, debris, and unwanted local fauna more than it was a high-speed armored vehicle, and it shrieked as it crumpled under the weight of the rover. Corin released the brakes and gave it more power, which kicked the back up and finished carrying the vehicle through and over the barricade.

Samuel had done his best not to notice the body of the staffer in orange that the rover plowed over. Hopefully, the man was already dead from one of Garn's bullets before the vehicle hit him. Once inside the compound he could see just how much damage the outlawed Fenrir weapon had done, and he understood why it had been so perfect for urban combat. The small caliber rounds were plenty capable of tearing through the unarmored bodies of the mining staff and yet did not possess the power or penetration capacity to do much if any, damage to the compound itself. All around them were the dying and the wounded, and Samuel realized there were far more than twenty people staffing this compound.

Garn had not actually killed very many people, though there were many wounded casualties scampering through the platform, fleeing in all directions from the merc squad suddenly in their midst. Narek wasted no time in disembarking. As soon as his boots hit the deck he'd already put a hot round through the back of a fleeing worker.

Samuel leaped out of the vehicle and was about to protest the shooting of unarmed people beyond what was necessary when several rounds peppered him, Narek, and the rover from the stairwell.

The marine's instincts took over, and before he realized what he was doing he took a knee and punched three tightly clustered rounds through the chest of a man wielding a pistol.

What hope the man thought he had of stopping such men as they Samuel could not fathom, though in the heat of battle strange things happened. Samuel stood and pushed inwards, heading towards the stairwell as he swept his rifle across the cowering forms of two other staffers. He'd seen cor-sec officers engage with pistols and shotguns against heavily armed gangers in the downspire of Vorhold. Having a weapon in hand made a person feel powerful, perhaps even invincible, especially if they were inexperienced with truly horrific combat. Shooting targets and unarmed civilians, perhaps the occasional poorly armed red lister, gave you no functional awareness of how pitifully outclassed you might be when faced with true killers.

Samuel raced up the stairs, eager to finish this fight and find his wife, especially if she was somewhere above and now rather likely engaged in her own contest of life and death. Jayce fell in behind him, the younger merc coldly executing two wounded staffers with his auto-pistol as he rushed to catch up with the marine.

Samuel nearly turned and shot Jayce himself, but focused on the task at hand. It had become painfully clear that none of the other mercs had any interest in the complexities and inconvenience of taking prisoners, as Samuel could hear the all-to-familiar report of Narek's Helion rifle spitting hot rounds into anyone he caught sight of. Garn and Michael were not far behind Jayce, with Corin and Narek bringing up the rear.

It was not lost on Samuel that despite Narek being the first off the Rover and into combat, he'd deftly positioned himself at the rear of the squad, while Samuel, in his haste, had become the tip of the spear. The marine shook off his frustration with the mercs and pulled his rifle tight into his shoulder. There would be time to balance accounts and redress offenses after he'd found his wife and they'd secured this damned compound.

Samuel emerged from the stairwell ready for battle, and instantly his iron sights were filled with targets. A man leaped into view and swung a blowtorch at Samuel, only to be stopped short and thrown backward by two tightly controlled bursts from the marine. Without pausing, Samuel kept running and twisted to the right so that he could punch several rounds through the groin and thigh of another pistol wielding security staffer, the man's chest armor doing him little good. The other mercs fanned out behind Samuel as the gunfire intensified.

Hard rounds slammed into the marine and he was knocked to the ground. His armor held, but he was temporarily shaken. From his vantage point on the ground, Samuel could see two rival mercs counter-attacking those from the *Rig*. Both of them were in full combat armor that looked to be of a decent make and carrying combat assault rifles with extended magazines. They poured on the fire, and suddenly a heavy weight fell on top of Samuel just as he was trying to get up.

Michael had been filled with holes, his affordable but flimsy patchwork suit of armor having done nothing to save him from the hail of bullets coming from the rival mercs. Jayce had sprinted to the right, disappearing into the maze of heavy support equipment for the drill mechanism on the platform above. Garn had taken cover behind a support strut, his empty machine gun discarded back in the rover and hands now filled with a stubby sub-machine gun that Samuel suspected had little hope of penetrating the enemy's armor.

"Draw them out, marine, I'm on the stairs," came the gravelly voice of Narek in Samuel's comm-bead, the order firm, and Samuel, ever the soldier, reacted just as much with the conditioning of a long military career as he did with conscious intent.

Samuel scampered left, after Jayce, but as he got to his feet he bracketed the two armored mercs with fire from his combat rifle. The Grotto rifle was a workhorse of a weapon, so while it did not quite have the penetration capacity to foil the enemy armor, it had plenty of knock-down power. One of the rival mercs stopped firing and evaded, disappearing behind one of the pieces of heavy machinery. The other staggered as he was hit, each round sending him further backward until suddenly he stepped into Narek's field of fire.

The former battle trooper squeezed the trigger and sent three super-charged hot rounds through the chest, neck, and head of the armored merc. The man went down twitching, his weapon clattering to the ground. Whoever owned this compound had most certainly chosen quality over quantity when it came to their mercs. While the man was no Merchant's Militant, for a non-union scab, the man had likely alone cost what the *Rig* was paying for at least two or perhaps three of the low rent mercs under Narek's command.

Samuel and Garn moved parallel to each other as they pursued the surviving rival merc into the thick maze of support machinery. This was the level just under the primary drill mount, and though Samuel desperately wanted to ascend the stairs and continue the search for his wife, this merc had to be dealt with. Considering his armor and weapons, the merc could easily circle back around and wipe them out, so there was no choice but to engage.

Hard rounds suddenly strafed across the platform, sending both Garn and Samuel to the deck as they hurled themselves out of the way. Narek cursed over the comm-bead, and Samuel couldn't help smiling as the former battle trooper could be heard clattering back down the stairwell after taking several rounds. The armored merc moved around the edge of a bank of power cells and sprayed more fire at Garn, who just barely managed to scamper his way to safety behind a large tool rack, the multiple impacts causing a storm of sparks to flash in the half-light of the platform.

The rival merc staggered backward as Samuel drove several rounds into his chest, giving Garn a moment's reprieve before ducking back behind a pylon.

The rival merc swept his gun around, spitting a hail of sustained fire as he did, and one round cut neatly through Samuel's armor and tore into the meat of his upper thigh. More rounds chewed away at the pylon as Samuel collapsed to the deck in pain and shock. He rolled onto his stomach and took aim, determined to at least return fire before he bled out or took another hit.

This time Samuel aimed for the rival merc's weapon instead of the man himself, and the device proved much less sturdy than the combat armor. The merc shouted in frustration and shock as the assault weapon was literally shot to pieces by the marine's sustained fire. Samuel's magazine clicked dry, and he saw the merc hastily cast away the shattered gun and attempt to flee. The rival merc had only gotten a few steps when Garn cut loose with his sub-machine gun, aiming at the merc's legs, the wave of projectiles doing nothing to penetrate the armor, though the multitude of impacts made the merc stumbled to the deck.

As Samuel struggled to his feet he saw Jayce materialize out of nowhere and empty his magazine at point-blank range into the back of the merc's helmet. The first handful of rounds did little, though as dents turned into holes, and then holes into a direct path to the merc's skull, it became the third execution Samuel had witnessed from the young merc. Samuel looked away and fumbled with his personal med kit, knowing that he needed to get a vial of anti-coagulant dumped onto his wound before he lost too much more blood.

By the time he had done so Jayce and Corbin rushed up the stairs towards the primary drill platform. Garn stopped to help Samuel after slapping a fresh magazine in his sub-machine gun, and the marine used the merc's support to steady himself before dosing with a stimulant. Samuel only had two of them in his personal kit, they were both holdovers from the war, and after so long their potency was somewhat reduced. Thankfully, in this particular situation, the diluted effect was a boon, as Samuel was able to ignore the pain enough to walk and still keep a clear head.

More shooting could be heard upstairs over the roar of the wind, and as Garn and Samuel reached the stairwell Narek rushed past them. Samuel could see that the former battle trooper's robotic arm hung limply at his side, which was also seeping blood from a rent in the armor. The arm was throwing sparks every few seconds, and Narek carried his rifle slung tightly across his shoulder so that he could fire from a half guard position with one hand. The marine waved Garn on, and as the uninjured merc took the stairs two at a time Samuel climbed up as swiftly as he could manage.

When he reached the top of the stairs Samuel pulled the stock of his rifle in tight against his shoulder and surveyed the scene before him. The platform was littered with bodies, and though not nearly so many as the two decks below, Samuel gave each corpse a moment's glace to ensure that it wasn't his wife. To his left he saw Narek turn and place five hot rounds through a piece of machinery, causing a corpse to fall behind it, a small pistol falling from its freshly slain hand.

Shapes moved in the dust and Samuel peered through his iron sights. His trigger discipline was immaculate, and when Captain Dar emerged from behind a stack of drill pipes the marine did not fire. He might have wanted to, angry as he was about the situation and the conduct of the mercs, though he did nothing. The marine lowered his weapon as Garn, Corbin, and Jayce swept the rest of the platform and moved to secure the topmost.

"Where is my wife, Captain?" snapped Samuel as he kept the muzzle of his rifle pointed down, even if not entirely away from the freelance prospector.

"I'm here, Samuel," answered Sura as she used the stack to support herself while walking around the pipes on legs made wobbly from her injury.

Samuel slung his rifle immediately and rushed to support his wife, and not a moment too soon, as her legs gave out just when he got his shoulder underneath her. The sudden extra weight on his legs gave him a fresh stab of pain from his own wound, though the marine gritted his teeth and bore it. Now that he was up close he could see that Sura had taken a nasty hit to the head, though her hair was matted from the blood to a point that he could not tell if she'd been hit with a blunt instrument or took a grazing shot from a bullet. She had Vol's gun in her hand, and there was blood drying on the blade.

"Drill secure!" came Narek's voice over the squad channel, and Samuel could see through the haze that Braden and Narek were now standing at the primary drill mount.

The geo-engineer was busy analyzing what appeared to be a fresh core sample, seemingly uncaring or unaware of the carnage that was strewn about. Soon the other three mercs came back down the stairs and gave a thumbs up to the former battle trooper serving as their squad leader. Garn appeared from the interior of the platform and did the same.

"Good work, everyone," said Captain Dar in a weary voice before casting his gaze around the assembled group, "Where's Michael?"

"We ran into some professional muscle downstairs," muttered Narek as he pinched a sparking cable on his robotic arm and bent it away from the other end of the severed line so that it ceased to throw sparks as it tried to send current. "Michael got retired. Shame."

"He pretty much ran straight into it if you asked me," smirked Jayce as he made a show of putting the safety back on his auto-pistol and fastening it to his chest mount, "Kinda surprised he lasted this long. Former cor-sec officers make bad mercs."

"Show some respect for the dead," growled Garn, bristling at the young merc's snide tone. Jayce held his hands up, palms out as he relented and went quiet.

"Everybody stow it," snapped Captain Dar, his voice cutting across the chatter as he activated his secondary transmitter to send a pulse signal to the *Rig Halo*. "Meridian will be here shortly. Let's get everyone with an injury to the rover and ready for dust off. Jayce, Corbin, and Garn police up the firearms tie up any loose ends, and pull security."

Dar offered to help Samuel get Sura down the stairs, as the woman was doing everything she could just to stay upright, and the pain of Samuel's wound was already making its way past the palliative drugs. Narek went down ahead of them, his weapon still active, sweeping from side to side as he scanned for survivors. None presented themselves on the second floor, and so the trio proceeded to the first. As they moved the geo-engineer rushed down the stairs after them.

"Primo stuff captain," said Braden, now out of breath, as he approached Dar and held up a tablet, "With just what they already have stockpiled we'll make a fortune. I haven't seen juice this good in years. Are you sure we can't work this play?"

"This ink-rock is going to be hard cargo until we can legitimize it at the exchange desk," answered Dar as he shook his head and nodded back up the stairs, "Get everything on the stockyard ready for pickup, I want this planet tasting our after burn in the next two hours."

Braden exhaled deeply and turned to walk back up the stairs.

"We just made fools of Ackerman and Jema on their own play, and the only reason we aren't taking air to surface fire from the Etheria right now is that they don't want to damage their own platform more than it already is," explained Dar as he looked at an incredulous Samuel, gesturing his head towards the carnage on the first floor. "They're making a bet that we'll seize the haul and leave. Then they can hire a new crew and start where they left off. It will cost them for sure, but people are cheaper than structures and equipment. If they fight us now, they'll lose more than they already have."

"Better to let us go than to risk losing the entire compound, or word getting out to other prospectors that they can't hold their own claim," observed Samuel as he grimaced in pain taking the last few steps down onto the hard-packed surface of the planet. "Which is also why they won't report this to any of the corporate authorities either. It was never the plan to work this play."

"You picked up on that pretty fast for a Grotto man," snorted Narek as he hauled himself up into the driver's seat of the rover with his good arm. "We hit em hard, take what's already been extracted, then get it to market with nobody the wiser. Exchange desk doesn't care where the juice comes from if there's nobody squawking, only that it arrives without a fuss."

"We've made an enemy, sure as sure, but this is necrospace, and the times we live in, Samuel," said Dar while he helped the marine get a still woozy Sura loaded into the rover, the captain noticing the grim look on the marine's face. "The cost of staking and defending our own claim, especially on a planet where there's a rival already drilling, would have been so much more than the cost of a raid. We risked big to do this, but the profit margin will be huge if we can get this to market before the next crash."

"We've become pirates!" snapped Samuel, his temper getting the better of him before he could force himself to keep quiet. Anger flashed briefly across Dar's face, but the captain maintained his calm.

"I told you the line was blurred, Samuel," said Sura suddenly, reminding the men in the rover that she was still at least semi-conscious. "Not much different than Reapers on a hostile salvage is it?"

"There are rules of engagement for salvage, or at least in theory," responded Samuel, his exasperation turning to exhaustion as the conversation continued. "And we killed everybody, no prisoners taken, just like pirates."

"Real pirates would do all that and then strip the compound after emptying the stockpile, but we 're leaving it intact," the captain added while Narek fired up the rover's engine and started backing the vehicle out so that they could get into an open landing zone for pickup. "Ackerman and Jema will have a new crew hired and be back into production in a few months, maybe even sooner. Though we've bloodied their nose, we didn't completely ruin them. There's at least some attention paid to sustainability here. Our own kind of trade war amongst prospectors."

"Tell that to Michael or all those prospectors we just retired. The new crew will be walking onto a compound with no clue how bad it went for the first one. Management on both sides mark the lives lost on the balance sheet and the drill keeps drilling. You're right captain," growled Samuel from the back seat as he looked back at the battle site, "Just like a trade war."

"I am losing my patience with your tone, Mister Hyst," stated Dar as a way of rebuttal while he turned in the passenger seat to face the marine, his own voice growing menacingly flat in the wake of the *Rig Halo*'s engines as the prospecting vessel appeared over the mountains and began its descent near the rover. "You perform a much-needed function on this crew and have been a great help to Yanna during production. I would be greatly displeased to find myself inclined to re-evaluate the decision to bring you and your family aboard my ship."

"Easy, Captain," said Sura with a strained voice as she squeezed Dar's shoulder and fought to remain conscious despite her desire to fall asleep, which she knew would be problematic given the high likelihood that she was suffering from a concussion. "You too, marine. This is the job, so let's finish it, shall we? We can argue about the details another time."

"Listen to the pretty lady, gentlemen," cackled Narek in his low voice, the former trooper seeming to find much humor in the strained relationship between the three passengers in the rover. "Paycheck over personality, as we say on Cressida, though I like your 'this is the job' thing, it's cute."

Narek made another comment, though the sound of it was drowned out by the roar of engines as the *Rig Halo* made its landing.

Samuel was furious, though he took several deep breaths and calmed himself down. He'd already been part of the atrocity and knew there was no taking it back. Sura was right, the only thing to do now was push forward, see to fruition what they'd set in motion. He'd never earned pay in his life that wasn't blood money of one sort or another, and though he yet wrestled with the brutal truth, it seemed unavoidable. The man who had once fought pirates had now become one himself.

ROCK LIFE

Samuel's goggles auto-tinted as he turned his head slowly to scan the topmost platform. The twin suns of UEP26 were beginning to drop behind the low mountain range, giving the unexplored planet's landscape a dull orange glow as the dusk light shone through the particle haze being ejected from the *Rig*.

The *Halo* hung in low orbit above the detached drilling compound, the silhouette of it looking almost more like a black beetle crawling across the atmosphere than a ship. Meridian had the vessel's weapons array primed as he took the craft on a long picket in order to maintain the security of the compound. From his vantage point, the pilot could swoop down hard and fire upon any incoming hostiles that were already in atmosphere or could hold the line against any coming in from the deep black of space.

It had been several years since the bloody events on Osi 2216, and while violence on that scale had not occurred since, the time had not passed without the occasional scrape.

Samuel had learned quickly that Captain Dar was indeed right, and the life of a prospector involved much more gunplay than the marine would have thought common. Any time Braden found a suitable planet to make a drilling venture there was about a half and half chance that there would either be squatters or prospectors already working a play or claim jumpers would emerge and make a run at the score before the *Rig Halo* was able to wrap up.

Narek proved himself a capable leader, more so than Samuel had initially estimated, and though the two men were often still at odds when it came to personality and the past, the security team functioned tightly. The former battle trooper had sent to Cressida for Michael's replacement, as well as another two shooters to bolster the ranks after the sudden departure of Jayce. The young merc had continued to show a particular lust for killing that eventually could not be ignored by the captain, though Samuel suspected it was Sura's voice in the Dar's ear that finally pushed him to cut the merc from the crew.

Samuel could not remember the names of the three new mercs, only Narek and Garn remaining in the forefront of his mind, and the marine found the lack of personal connection to the fresh recruits to be eerily similar to his time in the Baen Reaper Corps. Soldiers came and went, though it was only ever the ones that survived long enough whose name found its way into Samuel's memory. He quickly discovered that it was the same with Yanna's drill crew, as he spent just as much, if not more, time serving the drill master than he did Narek.

Yanna and her team were fast, and usually, the *Rig* was only deployed for a week or so before they'd extracted enough to cover costs, factor against the market flux, and yield sufficient profit margins to make it better than finding a different line of work.

Braden was good at finding the deposits, one of the best in the industry Samuel had come to find out, though even with such a genius aboard, the Halo spend more time docked or in the black than it did planetside. For every week or two on the ground, the crew would spend several months in the artificial gravity of the ship or one of the handful of stations to which the Halo paid docking subscriptions.

Samuel had spent plenty of time in the void as a Reaper and knew that to keep one's body fighting, and labor fit was a tremendous amount of work. Artificial gravity was all well and good, but the human body needed more, and so nearly every ship in civilization that was meant for deep runs came equipped with a gym of one size or another. While most everyone else had spent their childhoods planetside, his son, Orion's, young life had been lived just as much in the black as it had been on the surface of Baen 6 during his infancy and Longstride in his pre-teens. Now that he was a teenager, Samuel begrudgingly acknowledged, at the insistence of both Sura and, frustratingly, the captain himself, that the youth's body needed as much dirt time as it could get.

The light of the twin suns bounced off the patchwork Reaper's armor that protected Orion's body, and thanks to the helmet that covered his son's face, he looked just like any other salvage marine.

The years of homesteading on Longstride had paid off, and Orion was much larger and stronger than he would have been if he'd been raised in the half-lit urban stacks of Baen 6 like his father. The youth held the combat rifle in proper form, and his head moved slowly as he scanned the perimeter. Orion was only a few years younger than Samuel had been when he and Ben Takeda had first signed up for the Reaper Corps, and with Sura standing next to the young man, Samuel felt almost as if he were looking at himself from times past.

Sura was different to be sure, and not just because she was older than she had been when she and Samuel had met. She was thicker of shoulder and limb, which was just as much the result of hard work as it was exercise. Even the changes in her body weren't what struck Samuel as much as the way she moved, the way she dressed, and the rogue's demeanor that had crept into what had once been a bright personality.

While Samuel still kept his military bearing and somewhat reserved Grotto manner, Sura had fully embraced the onboard culture of the *Halo*, which was to say the greater culture of the prospectors, mercs, freelance colonists, and adventurers that made their life on the move and score to score. Her duster fell easily across her shoulders, and the combo revolver on her hip rested comfortably, ready to fill her hand with a faster draw than he'd even seen Vol or Boss Marsters manage.

Their relationship had been troubled from the start, and Samuel felt as if the wedge between them had first been driven in when he'd left for Reaper duty. They both had conducted their fair share of infidelity, and neither held it against the other. Life was hard in necrospace, and they'd each needed the comfort of another's embrace. It was in the past, and once Samuel reached Longstride they had enjoyed something of a romantic renaissance for a few precious years.

Osi 2216 had changed everything between them. Sura had known what they were heading into and chose to say nothing. For her, there was already an acceptance of the violent reality of life aboard the *Rig Halo*. While work had been relatively free of more conflict than the occasional skirmish to drive away competition or claim jumpers, the slaughter on 2216 stayed with Samuel.

He resented how swiftly and easily the crew of the *Rig Halo*, including Sura, were able to justify their actions. Samuel also resented his own hypocrisy, for while there indeed were theoretical rules of engagement for Reapers during hostile salvage, it had not always unfolded in such a clear-cut way.

More than once Reaper Hyst had found himself collecting base wages and hazard pay for battles in which he knew for certain he was not on the side of decency. For the crew of the *Halo,* there appeared to be little inner conflict, their callous pragmatism overcoming whatever emotional or ideological issues they might take with the implications of their actions.

As Samuel watched his son and his mother silhouetted in the dying light, he felt detached from them somehow. He would always be on the outside of their family unit. For so long it had just been Sura and Orion. Often it felt to Samuel that even when they were sharing the cramped quarters aboard the Halo, he was the odd one out.

Orion's accent was even changing, losing the Grotto to affect more and more of the spacefarer and station dweller patois. Not that Samuel was overly proud of his Grotto heritage, but it was a clear sign of how life aboard the *Halo* was changing Orion as much as it was Sura, perhaps more so.

Lately, Samuel had been thinking what life might have been like for Sura and Orion had he never returned. Would they have remained aboard the *Rig Halo* all this time or would Sura have pushed forward with the homestead on Longstride without him? Had he not been there, would the Tasca slavers have seized them? Part of Samuel wondered if the slavers would have even come to Longstride had he not been there, considering how eerily it was that the Gedra monster had been in the cargo hold. In the small hours of the night, when Samuel's sleep was troubled by a near certainty that the ghosts of Ellisian space had followed him home.

The thought of the Gedra, and what he had done in order to rid himself of the beast, snapped the marine out of his reverie.

The sun dipped behind the mountains, and in seconds the *Rig's* lighting flared to cast artificial illumination throughout the platforms and the ground beneath.

As uncomfortable as he was with Orion serving as part of Narek's security detail, at least the youth had learned much in the way of weapons and armor. While he had yet to kill anyone, much to Samuel's relief, the young man had become an acceptable marksman and could manage the armor at least as well as a Reaper fresh from boot camp.

It felt odd to Samuel as he turned and walked down to the drilling platform to return to work under the protection and weapons of his wife and son, though somehow, despite his grim mood, he felt comforted by their competency. If one of Yanna's drills snapped and the broken piece jumped its mooring to impale Samuel, he'd at least die knowing that they would be capable of surviving this kind of life, at least for as long as anyone could.

Samuel reached the bottom of the stairs and walked across the decking towards the center of the platform. The *Rig* was a rapid deployment drilling compound, almost identical to the one used by their competitors. It detached from the *Halo* and could be erected and operational within hours. However, even if the compound could be brought online so quickly, each play was different when it came to the drilling. They could be punching holes in the planet for days before striking juice, for while Braden could pinpoint the ink-rock, extracting it was not nearly so precise a science.

Yanna, the drill chief, insisted that it was just as much an art as it was a matter of engineering and technology. They were biting into unknown worlds, like mosquitoes on a new breed of creature, and it could sometimes take days for Yanna to find the right combination of drill bit style, metal composition, torque, and lubricant.

As it was, the thick hide of UEP26 proved to be a nasty blend of granite, iron, and a few other minerals that Samuel had never heard of. They'd already burned out one of their primary engines trying to break through, and while there were three backups, the first alone was already a costly setback.

Samuel approached the drill mount and saw Yanna, Braden, and one of the roustabouts installing one of the lighter drills.

"Well, don't you just look like a man with the weight of worlds on his shoulders," mused Yanna as a wide smile spread across her weatherworn features, revealing just as many laugh lines as worry lines. It reminding Samuel that he wasn't the only one to have seen so much of this scrapyard of a universe.

"I thought seeing a pretty sunset and getting some Vitamin D while we swapped out the bore pike for the juicer would do you some good. Seems to have had the opposite effect."

"Grotto people always look a bit dour," Samuel said as he cracked a half smile in spite of himself at the fact that pretty much every strong older woman reminded him in some way of Boss Maggie Taggart and if there was ever a voice to have over one's shoulder he could have done a lot worse. "I am also a little confused that you're fitting a juicer to the mount. I thought we were still trying to get through."

"The bore pike was sparking fires down there," answered Braden as he and Yanna clamped the bit into place. "Something about the composition of the pike and the unknown elements down there was interacting rather poorly. That's what pushed the engine out of commission."

"We're gonna have to go max spin on this bit, and since it's a softer metal it's going to need constant attention, Samuel. You're about to earn your keep in spades," said Yanna as she nodded to the roustabout. "James, set the board to red."

James moved to a control panel set into a nearby pylon and flipped several switches. As he did the ambient green lights that were positioned at each of the entries and exits to all of the different levels of the compound turned red. This let everyone working on the platform know that the drill was about to come online.

This was a risky time on the platform, for if any fatal accidents or catastrophic failures were to occur, it was during the actual drilling process. Most prospectors called it 'juicing' as opposed to drilling. For those who lived and died by the drill, there was a big difference between the threat level of the bore pike chewing through the outer layers of the planet crust and the juicer actually piercing the ink pockets. Ink-rock in its raw state was extremely volatile, and so when it was being extracted was the most dangerous time to be on the *Rig*. All work stopped as the pipeline crew below the primary drill platform steadied their equipment and the loaders on the stockyard ceased their preparation for the haul.

"Okay, boy, since we're using the juicer, that thing is going to pick up debris as soon as the temperature rises," said Yanna to Samuel as she took her place at the master station and began spinning the drill while Braden took his place at the station behind her in anticipation of taking samples of the ink once it began to flow. "I'm going to be riding the edge here, if I let the bit get too hot it'll lose structural integrity and we're all going to get a molten metal bath. You've got to be swift and damn precise to keep the debris from pressing in on the drill too much, and the more debris that stays the faster we cross our temp threshold."

"Well, I suppose if I fail to keep the drill sufficiently clean at least I'll be the first one to die," observed Samuel as he put on his welding helmet and lifted his Reaper's hand welder from the thong on his belt. "Seems fair."

Yanna laughed as an answer, and it was a good sound to hear. There was risk in everything they did as prospectors, and if a bullet wasn't coming then there were always errant power tools, exploding machinery, and unstable cash crops. During his time as a salvage marine there had been a great deal of injury, death, and danger, and yet through it all people like Ben Takeda and Harold Marr had been ready with dark humor. For the Reapers, the work of the torch was always preferable to the work of the gun, though at times it could be just as dangerous.

Samuel had learned the hard way that one did not always know what was waiting behind the airlock of a derelict spacecraft or just what may or may not be about to crash down or implode when he cut through a wall or bulkhead.

The marine ignited his hand welder, the symbol of the Grotto Reaper and easily the most important item his former lover, Bianca Kade, had allowed him to smuggle out when he left the Corps. His armor was more stout than the average enforcer or low rent merc, though compared to the battle troopers of Helion or the Merchants Militant, it was subpar. The combat rifle was a rugged workhorse of a weapon, though its utility was in its low maintenance requirements and reliability, not so much its knockdown power or ability to penetrate enemy armor. The Grotto hand welder, however, was state of the art, and no other corporation had yet to produce a more robust model. Grotto wasn't sharing either, and the fact that Samuel possessed both the welder itself and years of experience in its maintenance and use, made the marine a valuable asset to the *Rig*.

"We're going hot!" shouted Yanna, giving voice to her ritual saying before every drilling session even though everyone on the compound already knew thanks to the lights. "Let's poke a hole in this world and get paid!"

The whir of the drill was like a hurricane in Samuel's ears, even though he knew that half of that was his imagination, given that he was wearing protection. When the bit struck resistance, however, even the plugs and helmet could not keep out the screeching of metal against stone flecked with yet more metal. The entire platform rumbled from the contact, and the drill mount groaned against the torque. Samuel could see that their efforts were already yielding results, as the stacks attached to the back of the drill mount, leading out and away from the compound, began belching out particle clouds.

It occurred to Samuel that drilling operations like this were vastly inconsiderate when it came to pollution. Larger corporate compounds, backed by cor-sec and extended licenses, did not have to conduct the 'poke and go' plays of freelance prospectors. They were moderately more concerned with sustainability, and so spent the additional resources to collect the debris exhaust and re-filter it for secondary extraction. This yielded a larger ink-rock haul, and as a side effect caused a dramatically smaller amount of long-term pollution. After several days of extraction, this entire region of UEP26 would be blanketed in a low-grade toxic layer of ink-rock particles. This was to say nothing of whatever other metals, minerals, or compounds might be coming from beneath the surface, ground into a fine dust, and spread across the planet by prevailing winds. The crew of the Rig never stayed more than a few weeks on any one play, and never had to deal with the effects of exposure to the long-term effects of their extraction methods.

The screech of the drill changes suddenly, the high pitched keen becoming somewhat more throaty, and Samuel knew he was up. The drill was picking up debris, the metal getting hot enough that stone and metal below was melting. As the drill cycled up and down Samuel could see through the maintenance cage that large chunks of rapidly cooling material were attaching to the drill. He was suddenly reminded of the odd barnacles that appeared to grow within hours on the hulls of the scratch made boats he and the Reapers had used during the trade war. There was a depressing little world that had a wealth of edible algae that command had deemed worth fighting over, and during the course of the short campaign, Samuel had found himself burning off hundreds of the creatures.

The Grotto hand welder was small enough to be used inside the cage, which had barely enough room for Samuel as it was, much less the tanks and hoses of more traditional welders. The hand tool was also powerful enough to do the job, which would have been rather difficult for anyone less skilled in its use. Samuel not only had to be swift and precise with the application of the torch, he had to be deft enough not to burn away any of the drill bit itself.

Samuel took a deep breath, watched the drill long enough to pick up on its spinning rhythm, and then leaned in to do his work. The moment his torch, set to max burn, hit debris then molten rock and metal began sluicing away from the drill. There were catch pans affixed just below the cage. James and another roustabout were already switching out a filled pan with an empty one. It was dangerous work, both for Samuel and the roustabouts, and yet it was a process unique to the *Rig Halo*, made possible by Samuel's tools and expertise. Any other operation would have to just keep drilling until they'd either forced their way through the planet crust, torn apart all their pikes and juicers, or burned out all their spare engines.

Samuel entered something of a trance, all his focus zeroed in on the spinning metal and stone in front of him. The marine became unaware of the passage of time, his world shrinking down to the light of his torch and the swirling molten fluids splashing away from the drill and into the pans below. It was good to work, to have his finger on the trigger of a torch instead of a gun, and for a time, Samuel was at peace. Try as he might, the marine was still a man of Baen 6, and for all the struggle such an origin guaranteed, there was a begrudging love of labor that ran deep in Grotto culture.

Eventually, the drill bit through the last of the planet's physical resistance, and the cacophony of noise being emitted by the machinery died down to a low rumble. Moments later the molten rock and metal debris ceased to harass the drill, and Samuel stepped back from it as he shut off his torch. Yanna activated the juicer, and something that looked like a titanic hypodermic needle slid through the center of the still spinning drill. In the next few minutes, Samuel knew that the juicer would plunge into the tightly packed mass of ink-rock granules and start to suck them up.

Ink-rock was a strange and volatile material, functioning at times like a liquid and a solid, giving it physical properties similar to mercury. It tended to bead, even when mixed together with other ink-rock particles under pressure, and so when the particles began to flow up the juicer there was a rattle to it as if millions of glass marbles were flowing up the tube.

Samuel became aware of a cheer from the crew going across the comms channel, and he smiled in spite of his prior dark mood. The job, thus far, had gone smoothly. The marine knew better than to hope that every job could be like this, and in fact realized that most would likely not. Still, the marine walked back up the stairs with a lighter step than he'd come down with.

No combat, no gray areas, just a good play and honest work.

THE DAGDA

Dagda Station was a massive structure, one of only a handful this side of mapped space that possessed sufficient resource capacity and rugged design to occupy deep space coordinates. It resided just off the corporate shipping lanes, close enough to do a robust trade in official goods, but well positioned to entertain buyers and sellers from necrospace and the frontier who did not wish to attract corporate attention. While Dagda was owned and operated independently, like most stations outside the civilized core of mapped space, the corporations still had a presence in some capacity.

One of the benefits of corporate citizenship was the station and starport embassy system. As citizens moved through the universe they would always have some manner of lifeline to their parent company. Outside of the nasty business of a trade war, corporate citizens traveling outside the marked territory of their company could remain connected.

It was no different on Dagda, even if its position in the black gave it a dubious, even if well deserved, reputation for generating just as much illegal revenue as it did official revenue. The Bottom Line passed no judgment so long as the flow of commerce was strong, and where there was revenue the corporate interests found ways to mingle with independent elements. Even Grotto Corp, with its reputation for isolationism, maintained an embassy and exchange desk for modest hauls on board Dagda.

As the station's docking clamps gently shook the *Halo*, Sura missed the weight of the combo revolver on her hip, the mighty weapon now resting in its holster, slung from a peg on the wall in the cramped quarters she shared with Samuel and Orion. It had been a long time since she'd needed to use it on an enemy, and for that, Sura was thankful but more than a little bored. The last several plays had been uneventful, at least for her.

Narek's security team, with Samuel's help, had become a rather effective deterrent when it came to scavengers and claim jumpers.

Despite Dar's best attempts at discretion and assurances of the same from Ackerman and Jemma, word had gotten around about the Osi massacre several years back. These days when the *Rig Halo* broadcast its ident codes, most prospectors competing for a play would back off without a fight, and claim jumpers would pass them by for a less difficult score when the *Rig* was already drilling.

Sura's job on board the ship had transformed into her being somewhere along the lines of Dar's second. While she commanded no official authority, the crew had begun to treat her like a first mate. She and the captain had grown closer, and part of that made functioning as a de facto first mate feel natural for her. The crew respected her, and she found that, for the first time in all her years, she had something approaching control over her own life. No longer was she drifting from life raft to life raft, daydreaming about the future and waiting for her husband to return home. Her presence meant something on the *Rig Halo*, and as they hunted for their prizes amid the black of space and on the dirt of alien worlds, she felt good about herself.

Now that their reputation preceded them, for good or ill, the process of boarding stations and selling their haul at the various exchange desks was much less complicated. Clerks in the know were much less inclined to drive the hard bargain. So, too, were the various criminal elements stationside, for while there were technically no firearms allowed on the station other than those carried by the security staffers, this was necrospace after all and small caliber pistols were a reality station side, even if officially banned.

There was a multitude of ways the crew of the *Halo* could be relieved of their cargo or their lives while docked. However, these days even the bad men of most stations avoided plotting any schemes against the *Halo*. Not after the Captain had used his not infamous sword to run through several bravo toughs on Andromeda a year ago, long before that Red List raiding party nearly killed the station.

Now that the massacre was common knowledge, nobody tried anything, dirt side or on the station, and though she knew it was insane to wish for conflict, Sura was getting restless.

The woman let herself feel the reassuring presence of the slim pistol resting in a pocket sewn into the lining of her duster. The bullets were tiny and incapable of penetrating armor or, more importantly, the station's hull, though they packed enough of a punch to tear up flesh. Security staffers, especially those who enjoyed the occasional free drink or cash tip from the captain, tended to care little about such low-grade weapons. So long as the spacefarers and station thugs kept the violence to a minimum, off the beaten path, and caused no structural damage, the security staffers rarely risked their own lives to do much policing. They stuck to the central deck, the prime market at the core of the station where corporate business was done, and much of the rest of the deep space community was a frontier of corridors and chambers intentionally left to the flourishing black market.

"You're looking rather predatory this evening, Mrs. Hyst," smirked Captain Dar as he walked beside Sura, his sword hanging from his belt and a data tablet containing the full account of their UEP26 haul. "Maybe tone it down a bit until we've collected and have money to lose. The clerks are nervous enough as it is around us these days."

"I am just on edge is all," said Sura as she gently took a deep breath and exhaled, visibly relaxing, though still feeling somewhat coiled. "Pent-up energy. I'm just glad to be off the boat for a bit."

"I know we agreed not to talk about it, but are you and Samuel okay?" began Dar, his usual bravado suddenly evaporating, leaving behind a softening of his features and a nervousness in his voice, something Sura had learned was a reaction unique to her, and thus frustratingly endearing. "There's been talk. Thin walls on board ship, as they say."

Sura turned to look at Dar and quickly looked away again. The expression on his face was of genuine concern and considering the years of silent angst and competition between this man and her husband, she knew it cost him some of his pride to ask.

The relationship between her, Dar, and Samuel had been a strained one, though of late, Sura had found herself withdrawing from both men, despite living with one and growing closer to the other in a professional capacity. There had always been something between her and the captain, ever since that first chance meeting on Pier 13, and they both knew that had Samuel died in the trade war they'd have chosen to be a couple many years ago.

We would have been a good one too, thought Sura as her face flushed and she looked ahead at the sliding door leading to the central deck, *but I made a promise.*

"It's been hard, Felix," answered Sura, her use of his first name making the captain inhale sharply, as she had not used his first name in a long time, not since she told him years ago that whatever was between them could never be. "I lied to him about the plan on Osi, we've not been the same since. More like angry bunkmates going through the motions. When there's action I can ignore what life has become."

Captain Dar said nothing and looked away as he composed himself. The prospector opened the sliding door that led to the central deck, and the pair let the sights, sounds, and smells wash over them as they stepped out onto the platform. The two of them stood silently for a moment, taking it all in. After months on board the confines of the *Rig Halo*, docking at a station so vibrant and dangerous as Dagda was a balm for both of them.

"Mother, this is incredible!" breathed Orion as he, Braden, and Corbin marched up behind them.

Sura looked back and smiled, the sight of her son's wonderment banishing the grim mood that had been consuming her.

While Samuel was too paranoid to leave the ship, a sentiment shared by the captain who thought it best for him to remain unknown and unseen, Sura had been boarding stations for years since their flight from Longstride without incident. As the unofficial first mate, she was present for the captain's deals with the exchange desk, and though she'd not had to fight on a station thus far, part of her job was to be ready to do so. As for Orion, this was his first time to Dagda. While he'd been off the ship, much to his father's chagrin, a few times on the smaller orbitals, never had he encountered the wilderness of a vast station such as this.

Orion's eyes widened as a table girl, named Dagda, no doubt, slid her gaze up and down his body as she waltzed past the small group. The youth's head turned to follow her, and his cheeks flushed. Sura realized, quite suddenly, that the only women he'd seen in his life were of the hardier frontier sort. While attractiveness was a relative term, she couldn't blame Orion for gawking as the table girl was indeed beautiful, and the way she moved was professionally calculated to get a rise out of any onlookers who might be ready to spend the coin.

No sooner had she gone down the stairs to the next platform did a rough looking long hauler shout over to her and wave his credit pass. In an instant, the young woman had eyes only for her client, and moments later she allowed the long hauler to wrap his arm around her waist and escort her through one of the many hatches adorning the central platform.

"Stay close, Orion, this place has just as many predators as it does pretty things," said the captain as he put a hand on the youth's shoulder and pulled him along with the group while they began walking in the opposite direction. "Let us do the talking and don't accept anything someone offers you without me or your mother giving you the nod. It's an adventure sure as sure, just have to be careful."

The group moved through the central deck, and Sura was forced to smile as Orion's mind was opened to the vast sights and sounds of the station. The current exchange rates for a plethora of raw materials were displayed on a multitude of screens, some inlaid into the wall and others affixed to the railing, throughout the deck. Competition was just as fierce on the station as it was out in the black, and each of the corporate exchange desks was constantly changing their rates in an endless stream of shifting data.

Every few seconds the Helion rate for ink-rock would dip below that of Grotto, only to be beaten by Rubicon in a race to the bottom. Before the rates went in the negative and the market crashed, something that would take weeks or even months for everyone to recover from, the rates would skyrocket as the corporations backed off and allowed stability to return.

Sura recalled from her time in Grotto that the enigmatic and aloof order of corporate masters known as the Anointed Actuaries were behind Grotto's market efforts. While she had never seen one in the flesh, like the vast majority of all other Grotto citizens current or former, her husband had. Samuel described the Actuary as only barely human, more machine than man, and she could imagine a cyborg on some distant planet playing with numbers, steering the course of billions of lives with contracts and decimal points.

Captain Dar was intentionally taking the long way through the central deck, Sura realized, giving Orion what amounted to the full tour. She caught Dar's eye and silently mouthed a thank you, eliciting a wink from the man as he went back to explaining why bounty scrappers were called vultures and going on about the finer points of artificial gravity drives on the station. They were moving towards the Helion exchange desk, which Braden insisted had the most consistent rate.

As it turned out, Rubicon had the rate which yielded the most profit, and by a thin enough margin that a few minutes after the deal was made the rate shifted to a loss for the corporate desk. The clerk simply shrugged, as the rate would shift again soon enough, and by the time the ink-rock from UE26 was off-loaded from the *Halo* and stacked in Rubicon's own hauler the margin could fall in the corporation's favor once more. That was a constant risk that the corporate elements could afford to endure, and a loss today could be made up with a gain tomorrow, though for the prospectors a loss today meant that the chances for a tomorrow at all were slim.

With the deal done, but the cargo still changing hands, the captain decided it was time to give Orion a taste of station food and perhaps something stronger than recycled water. Sura knew Samuel would disagree, though the marine was busy with Meridian offloading the ink-rock and making sure Rubicon got everything they paid for. Dar's tablet would chime when the exchange was complete and full payment transferred, so until then it appeared there would be little harm in taking a moment to enjoy the station.

Sura was soon seated at a modest eatery at the bottom level of the core deck, sipping a powerfully lemon flavored liquid from a small metal cup not much larger than a thimble. She watched and smiled as Orion did his best to be polite about the food. Captain Dar had been living and working in the black for so long he'd forgotten just how vibrant and delicious food harvested in real gravity from real dirt could be.

Orion had certainly spent his early childhood eating the reconstituted station food aboard Pier 13, and the bland processed meals of Grotto when they were still living on Baen 6, though his formative years had been on Longstride. The youth had grown his own vegetables, hunted his own game meat, and knew what real home cooked food had the potential to be.

For all the joy she'd felt at his first glimpse of the Dagda, there was a bittersweet core, for she knew that so long as they were spacefarers what meals they could have here were likely the best he'd ever have again. Orion was making a show of enjoying a slice of re-hydrated meat even as Dar was unknowingly making a fool out of himself by going on and on about the quality of a spear of re-hydrated asparagus, and Sura couldn't help but feel a warmth spread through her as she watched them. Dar would never replace Samuel, but the bond between the captain and the youth was strong; Dar had been there for the boy during several of the years while Samuel was off at war.

"Well, isn't this a charming picture," sneered a voice. Suddenly, Jayce unceremoniously slid back a chair and seated himself at the table along with them, his sudden presence seeming to suck all the air out of the immediate area, his smile hollow and his eyes burning with malice, "It's like you don't know what's happened."

For a moment nothing was said, as Jayce moved his piercing gaze from Sura to Orion, and finally to Dar. It had been a few years since they'd dropped him, and while it was perfectly reasonable that he might find work that would bring him to the station, he had the look of a predator in his eyes.

The merc made a show of taking the metal cup of lemon liquid that Orion had not yet had the courage to touch and tossed the contents into his mouth.

His other hand was under the table, and as he swallowed the distinct sound of a slide being racked made everyone go still. He'd chambered a round and left the slide open in order to make that very gesture, and he now had their rapt attention.

Sura could see out of the corner of her eye that three other rough looking men, presumably compatriots of Jayce, had taken seats at the other table with Braden and Corbin.

"The only major event I am aware of is the fact that you have joined us uninvited, Jayce Rinn," uttered Captain Dar in a low steely voice, his usual bright demeanor gone cold as he took a sip of the hoppy station grog from a personalized chalice he usually carried on a belt loop. "I bear you no ill-will, and removing you from the crew was just business. I would be disappointed to make this personal."

"You left me on Cressida with a decent severance, so I got no quarrel with you. I wouldn't come all the way out to the Dagda just to feud with a bunch of prospectors anyway, though I'm glad your choice in ports is still somewhat predictable. I figured it was a fifty-fifty chance you'd offload here or on Taloc," snarled Jayce through a false smile. He set the tiny cup down and produced a data tablet from his jacket, which he activated and slid across the small table to Dar. "Oh, Captain, my Captain, I don't give a spit about you or your crew, that was just a job. This is an opportunity."

Captain Dar said nothing as he read what was on the tablet. Sura watched him closely, not daring to make eye contact with Jayce. She'd felt uncomfortable around him from the start, and though it had taken much in the way of private insistence with the captain, she was only too happy to see the merc cut from the crew. The others that replaced him might not be that much better, but there was a difference between killing for pay and killing for pleasure, and she knew Jayce was the sort of man who relished both.

Suddenly, Dar's expression darkened, and he sighed deeply as he set the tablet on the table and slowly, deliberately, pushed it over to Sura.

"Before anything else is said, Jayce, give her a moment to read," growled Dar in a voice that broached no argument. "She must know what is at stake."

Jayce simply kept smiling, and as Sura picked up the tablet. She almost felt like he was more excited for her to read than the captain. It was an acquisition order, a request for the forcible recovery of a human asset, issued by Grotto Corporation. However, it was not an internal order, instead, it was being openly offered to any recovery element of sufficient capacity to apprehend, detain, and transport the asset. So Jayce was on Dagda as a bounty hunter, and why he would be coming at them in such a threatening manner was beyond her.

Then she read the name of the human asset.

Samuel Hyst.

"That's right, pretty eyes," snarled Jayce, and just as Sura reached into her duster and put her hand round the grip of her pistol she found the muzzle of Jayce's weapon pressed painfully under her ribs. "Easy now. Don't think I won't drop you right here, bitch. Sammy has a wife *and* a son, I only need one of you to make this go my way."

"Sura, please," said Dar, his eyes pleading as he held his hand flat against the table, palm up, "He won't do anything we don't make him do. Let's be reasonable."

"What?" asked Sura, not moving her hand away from her pistol, though remaining still in spite of the fact that Jayce kept pressing the pistol harder into her side.

"Ain't it obvious?" cooed Jayce as he leaned in closer to Sura but kept his eyes on Dar, his breath sending prickles up her spine as he spoke. "Your Reaper goes without a fuss and his family doesn't have to die."

Everyone was silent, the captain staring daggers at Jayce and Sura doing her best not to make eye contact with anyone. A storm raged in her mind. She didn't trust herself not to spring into action if she met the gaze of Orion or Dar. The captain broke the silence after a moment's pause.

"Jayce, this can be done without blood. If a low rent merc like you is holding a Grotto acquisition order then that means you have a sponsor who brokered the lead, so your cut is already reduced, no sense in risking any more of what's left," said the captain, which got a sharp intake of air from Sura even as his statement seemed to visibly ease Jayce.

"Then we have an understanding," smiled the mercenary turned bounty hunter.

"If it's not you then someone else will come along," sighed Dar, his cold expression now turned to fatigue.

Sura locked eyes with the captain. "Just like that?" she rasped through gritted teeth, her blood boiling.

"He's right, you know. That's an acquisition order from one of the Grotto Anointed. It came through about a week ago. You'll have every bounty hunter and enforcer in mapped space looking for him, and for a reward that big they'll never stop," Jayce explained matter-of-factly, in syrupy tones, as he slid a blade from his hip and held it in reverse against his forearm before putting his arm on the table, hiding the knife from sight but making sure that Sura and the captain knew it was there. "So why don't you drop the hard cargo and fly away with no worries. You and the captain here can cut through all that sexual tension once and for all."

Captain Dar's eyes went wide, and Sura knew he was about to do something stupid, his sudden rage at the insult having gotten the best of him. The captain sucked in his breath and turned his palms over. Jayce tensed and Sura prepared herself to attempt pushing him away to foil the merc's point-blank shot.

However, before any of those seated at the table could make a move, the dim half-light of the platform was bathed in an orange glow.

"Samuel Hyst, you are bound by law to stand down!" boomed an amplified voice.

Out of the shadows emerged an armored figure, his body shining with inlaid orange lights that reflected off the growling force shotgun that was leveled at Orion.

"Submit!"

INSTRUMENTS OF FEAR

Recovery Agent Trask was well aware that the young man in front of him was not Samuel Hyst but in fact the former Reaper's only known offspring. The resemblance was sufficiently strong enough that as long as Orion was apprehended the transient population of Dagda Station would accept the ruse as reality. The tactical situation in the half-light of the lower deck was far from ideal, though the agent had to admit that it made for an impressive display of Grotto's reach and power.

Recovery actions on bustling stations and starports were what brought in the bonuses and kept people in line. Better to take the skippers in public and make a spectacle of it than to bag them clean where nobody could see. In this case, Trask was going to have to conduct the recovery in chapters, and while that annoyed him deeply, the agent was positive that there was no team better suited for the mission.

The acquisition order had come through on all Grotto channels, and though this Samuel Hyst wasn't a bond skipper, Trask would be damned if some bounty hunter cost Grotto the sum of the reward.

As Trask leveled his force shotgun at the young man, he actually wanted to blast the smarmy merc instead, the sneering trigger man having swiftly become a symbol of everything Trask hated about this entire scenario. The idea of mercenaries and bounty hunters with no loyalty to Grotto Corporation seizing the reward was beyond offensive to him. Grotto took care of its own problems, and his team was part of that process.

While the former Reaper, Samuel Hyst, had no outstanding debts to Grotto, the Anointed had marked him as a fugitive and backed it up with a small fortune in offered reward. Upon receiving the order Trask had researched this salvage marine and discovered a man who had been no friend of Grotto from graduation onwards, even if he had done his job and paid his debts.

Hyst's service record was impressive, and to Trask, he'd have been a hero of the corporation had he not also been instrumental in the Reaper Strike and subsequent union movement that was even, to this day, causing all sorts of complications and civil unrest inside the company. People's lives were being destroyed all across Grotto space, as events like the union uprising on Trigag were replayed over and over. Things were better when people knew their place, and Trask was passionate about his duty in seeing that the people of Dagda Station were reminded of theirs.

"Samuel Hyst, you are bound by law to stand down!" bellowed Trask once more as he marched towards the table, taking note that Lovat was coming up on their flank, while Aeomi kept to the shadows as backup. "Submit!"

"No easy money," stated Jayce, the smile never leaving his face, his voice steady, and then everyone at the table exploded into action.

Jayce leaped from his chair, diving to the right as he sprayed hastily aimed pistol fire at the oncoming armored agent. Sura twisted her body away from where the pistol had been a moment before, expecting the point-blank shot, only to be pushed back into her chair as the merc slammed his blade into her chest while he turned to fire on the agent. Dar flipped the table to the side to clear a path between him and Sura.

An instant later the table exploded into splinters as the energy discharge from Trask's weapon disintegrated it. The force of the blast was radically dissipated, though Dar was still thrown from his lunge into Orion, who had been rising from his seat, and both of them went sprawling across the deck.

Trask dove to the left, hurling himself away from the withering pistol fire. His armor could handle the bullets, though the sheer multitude of impacts made him stumble and careen into another table of fleeing patrons. The agent was used to getting shot at, even being hit, though he was getting older, nearing retirement in fact, and the punishing salvo got the better of him. More bullets chewed up the deck around him as yet more thumped into his chest and legs. The agent was surprised that the merc had been able to smuggle a full-auto machine pistol onto the station, and he regretted that the man had seemed not to care about the bystanders he was gunning down in the process.

That was always a risk in such deadly recovery actions. The job of the agent was to make the apprehension as much of a spectacle as possible, but without causing so much collateral damage that the population's fear turned to anger. Countless times he'd made the approach, used his voice caster to shout out the name of his prey and insist they stand down, and countless times the skipper took a knee and that was it. When the skippers fought back, things usually got nasty, and though Trask had yet to fail to bring in his collar, it had been years since the shootout with the Chiodo brothers, and he'd forgotten how rough such actions could be.

For as blindingly fast as the merc was, faster than the agent had ever seen, the trigger man hadn't noticed Lovat, having suffered from the kind of bloodthirsty tunnel vision such bravos often did. As the merc's pistol went empty and he began to slap in a fresh magazine his body was picked up and hurled onto the deck by a blast from Lovat's force pistol. The former warden-turned-agent's armor was ignited as he plowed through fleeing bystanders and fired once more, the second shot barely missing Orion as the captain shoved the boy aside.

Trask rose to a knee as he took note of Orion's comrades at the other table. One of the prospectors, the older one, lay in a growing pool of blood upon the deck, having been shot several times at point-blank range. There were three men backing away from the upturned table, chairs, and corpse, each firing in a different direction. Two of them were mercs who had initially approached the prospectors, and as one fired his pistol at Lovat, the other used his pistol to drive the surviving prospector into cover as they exchanged haphazard salvos.

Trask racked the slide of his shotgun and charged from his crouching position as he fired at the closest merc, the one shooting at the prospector. The blast caught the merc full in the chest and sent him sailing into the crowd. The discharge would not kill him, though he'd have enough broken ribs and internal bruising that he wouldn't be getting up anytime soon. Trask saw Orion rushing to his mother, who still sat in her chair, slumped over and unmoving. Before he could pump his shotgun and drop the lad several rounds bit into his side, this time one of them penetrated the armor, as the prospector rose from cover with a large caliber pistol and a determined look on his face.

"Aeomi, *now!*" shouted Trask, his voice tight with pain as he turned to take a knee while firing his shotgun. The blast shattered a food stall, barely missing the prospector as he scrambled out of the way. Trask was beginning to suspect he might be a merc who rode with the prospectors as security.

Aeomi leaped from her perch on one of the platforms above, using a rappelling line attached to the bottom of Raptor Two, which now hovered above them, to control her descent. The recovery agents had laid this trap when Aeomi caught the scents of Orion and Sura.

Given the Halo's sales records with the exchange desk, Trask had narrowed down the number of stations and market colonies where the Halo might appear to offload their next haul. The agents had held their position for nearly a week, posing as civilians taking a bit of R & R from life in the black. Time had grown short, though from the first moment the prospectors entered the central deck Aeomi had picked up their scent, and the agents scrambled to put their plan into action.

Trask and his team had been close to the frontier, having just dropped a collar off with an Aegis headhunter who bought out the bond of their prey and intended to make a vulture bounty scrapper out of him. Based on the information in the acquisition order, which went to Grotto channels a full week before it was disseminated to outside sources, it had not been difficult to find the dilapidated homestead that the Hyst family had once occupied.

While every other bounty hunter and enforcer was combing through nav logs and passenger manifests, Aeomi had familiarized herself with the scent of the Hysts. In this technological age, it was the raw senses of a born hunter that had given Trask's team the edge.

Aeomi landed hard right behind Orion, and instead of attempting to draw her pistol and shoot him she closed in and put the youth into a grinding sleeper hold. With her arms constricting his blood and oxygen, she kicked his knee out from under him and the boy was out in seconds. As he fell to the ground Aeomi swiftly affixed mag-clamps around the boy's wrists, and then a moment later slapped a carabiner across the center of the clamps. The carabiner was attached to the same rappel line Aeomi used to descend, and the moment she put it into place it drew taunt as the drone hovered above. With practiced grace and professional alacrity, Aeomi stepped back and tapped a command into her wrist module, and a moment later Raptor Two began to lift Orion off the ground.

Trask fired one more shot at the merc, missing again, though successfully keeping the man engaged. Trask saw out of the corner of his eye that Lovat had put down one of the other mercs. That was when the agent saw a flash of steel and turned just in time to see Captain Dar thrust the blade of his sword through the remaining mercenary's torso. The captain was shouting into his comms as he slid the blade free, before firing a pistol he must have pulled from one of the dead men with his off hand at Lovat. The warden went down hard, though Trask could see him moving moments later, wounded but still in the fight.

The captain moved to engage Trask, though his attention shifted upwards as Orion's unconscious form rocketed into the air, with Aeomi holding onto the mag-clamp with one hand and rising as well. The captain shouted and fired the remaining two bullets in his pistol at the drone, though they pinged off its armor and did nothing to hamper its rise. The captain screamed and hurled his pistol in frustration before being knocked to the ground by Aeomi's force pistol as she took a long-range shot. It wouldn't put him down for long, but it bought the agents a moment's reprieve.

"Lovat on me!" shouted Trask the moment he saw that Orion was firmly in the clutches of Raptor Two and sailing up the central deck towards the pre-established rally point.

Trask fired one more shot at the prospector merc, this time taking out the cargo crate he'd been hiding behind and knocking him to the ground, leaving him temporarily stunned and giving Lovat enough time to sprint towards the maintenance hatch that the team had planned for use in making their exit. Lovat had become quite the slicer and had been able to bypass the mechanized lock without being noticed by the station's own security forces.

In seconds this place would be crawling with first responders, and while the agents were righteous in their execution of an acquisition order, they were far from Grotto space and so there was no expectation of reliable assistance. If local security wanted to challenge them, the agents would either have to fight or bribe their way out of there and back into Grotto space. Might made right on the ragged edges of necrospace, and no corporate authority would do them any good this far out.

Trask and Lovat pounded through the maintenance corridor, having memorized the most direct path to their ship. Above them, Aeomi would soon be shutting down the drone and putting it on a grav-lift alongside Orion. She would move through another maintenance corridor that opened up onto one of the five hangar decks, where *Recovery Ship 78* awaited their return. The wound in Trask's sideburned, and he knew he was losing a decent amount of blood. Lovat too was wheezing badly, and Trask could see that the former warden had taken that shot from the captain in his left lung.

"I sound like you did back on Post 47, wheezing like an old man," joked Lovat through a grimace of pain as he struggled to keep up with his superior. "I hope your plan works Boss, we haven't gotten this beat up since the Chiodo brothers."

"It will," assured Trask as they pointed their weapons at a pair of tech staff who went scampering in the other direction.

"I wish we'd been able to keep that merc from stabbing Hyst's wife," admitted Lovat, his voice low and if it wasn't for their shared comms system Trask might not have heard it over the sound of their armored boots stomping over the deck as they rushed to their ship. "I read the files on our collar for once, shocker, I know, but damn has that family been through some hard times."

Trask stayed silent, choosing to say nothing, as there was little of value in any words he might use. Sura Hyst had been the key to his swift investigation, and he felt awful that she'd met such a poor end. She had survived the massacre on Pier 13 somehow and disappeared for several years afterward. When she resurfaced it was to purchase and license the homestead on Longstride.

She had found some way of maintaining an income to achieve the funds required to make such a large purchase, and since she'd been off the grid for so long it stood to reason that she was making her way in the black amongst the spacefarers. It was only a process of elimination to determine which of the handful of ships that escaped the brutal fighting on Pier 13 was still active and in operation.

There were twenty ships upon which Sura Hyst could have earned a reliable living, and considering how common it was for such operations to use multiple idents, Trask counted it as an old agent's intuition that he had pegged the *Rig Halo* as the most likely berth. If she had a good relationship with the captain and crew of the prospector ship, then when the Hyst family made a run for it, the *Halo* was likely the only ship out there who could have made them disappear so swiftly and kept them hidden for so many years.

Not that anyone had been looking for them until now, and Trask had to admit that he should have expected other hunters to have come upon the prey just as quickly as he and his team.

From the snippets of conversation he'd picked up, it seemed that there had been some uncomfortable history between the roguish merc and the prospector crew. At least the presence of the mercs made for a spectacle, even if Trask was saddened by the untold bystander casualties, and like Lovat, after pouring over the life and times of the Hyst family, he felt sick that Sura's journey had ended in such a way. His intent had been to capture her as well as Orion, though perhaps there was yet something to salvage, based on the captain's reaction to her demise.

Lovat and Trask soon exited the maintenance hatch and found Aeomi already in the process of loading Orion and the drone onto *Recovery Ship 78*. Costly and violent as it had been, the agents had what they'd come for, and without running afoul of station security or tipping their hand to any other hunters before the trap was sprung.

Now it was a matter of Samuel Hyst making the next right move because if he did not, the armed and dangerous people around him would.

LOST IN SPACE

"Hyst get your fangs out!" shouted Narek as he stomped down the *Halo*'s loading ramp and slammed his booted feet against the deck of the docking platform, "We've got incoming!"

Samuel dropped the handle of the grav-lift full of ink-rock containers he'd been steering and yanked the combo revolver from the holster on his hip. Sura usually carried the heavy weapon, but since no such obvious firepower was allowed on the station proper she'd been forced to leave it behind.

Each cargo platform was something like neutral ground between the docking ship and the Dagda, and for the sake of propriety, spacefarers were not restricted here. The security of cargo and a non-violent exchange was important to the masters of the station, and having an armed crew invested in everything going smoothly made the job of the security teams all the easier.

No sooner had Samuel cleared leather than a man in patchwork armor emerged from the main entrance hatch and started firing with what appeared to be a small bull-pup assault rifle. It reminded Samuel of the sort of weapons he had seen carried by cor-sec armsmen on board the larger corporate vessels. It fired special Fenrir, Inc. bullets often called "deck rounds" and was one of the more popular weapons among those who had to fight inside pressurized spacecraft. The rounds had a solid kick behind them when they were fired, but the projectiles themselves were made of an exceptionally soft metal. This way the bullets would either flatten out against armor or hulls without causing any collateral damage to the station, but would tear through flesh easily.

Samuel wasn't wearing any armor today, unfortunately, just the usual flight suit he wore for non-combat assignments. He leaped for cover just before a flurry of bullets spanked into the deck, side of the ship, and the, thankfully, thick hides of the ink-rock containers.

The Rubicon desk rep was not as swift to react, and when the man with the assault rifle tracked Samuel with his fire the rep's body was stitched with four rounds across the torso before he realized quite what was happening.

The bark of Narek's Helion battle rifle cut through Samuel's awareness, and just as he rose to lend his fire to the former trooper's he saw another hostile individual rush through the hatch and pitch something into the air. At the last second, the marine realized what it was and shielded his eyes. The thrown object turned out to be a flash grenade, and as soon as it detonated, Samuel heard Narek start cursing. Meridian, the ship's pilot, was crouched down behind his own overturned grav-lift, which was already shot to pieces, and if he stayed there a moment longer he'd be dead.

Samuel pulled back the hammer of the combo revolver and pulled the cylinder full of standard rounds to swap it out with one of his other speed loaders. In the time it took him to do that he could hear Narek continuing to shout angrily as he laid down suppressing fire. He might be blind, but he knew that if he didn't pour it on, the enemy would have a chance to drop him. Samuel saw more bullets tear apart the overturned grav-lift, and two bit into Meridian's left calf as he tried to sprint away.

The marine crouched low as he came around the other side of his lift and leveled the heavy revolver at the man with the assault rifle. In the span of a breath, he was able to see that the man's patchwork armor wasn't actually as patchwork as he'd initially thought, instead it was a solid suit with rags hanging over it, masking the quality for all but the most knowledgeable of observers.

Mercs, and better than the sort Dar could afford.

Samuel squeezed the trigger of the revolver, and a homemade explosive round knocked the merc off his feet as it exploded against his chest plate. The wildcat ammunition was worth the money Samuel had paid for it, and thanks to the rugged nature of the ganger weapon it could fire all manner of rounds without fail. Samuel swept his weapon to the side and fired again at the merc who'd thrown the flash, though his shot went wide and blew a chunk of metal and wiring out of the opposite wall.

The marine's opening shots were enough to buy Meridian time to scamper up the plank and into the *Halo*. A third armored mercenary started shooting at Narek from the elevated dock master's platform, drawing Samuel's attention away from the gunfight erupting between the last of two surviving Rubicon cor-sec staffers who had the misfortune of drawing duty on the *Rig Halo* delivery. The cor-sec staffers were only armed with station pistols, small caliber weapons that were standard issue on Dagda, and though the staffer was able to score several hits against the merc who assailed him, the stout armor stopped them all.

Samuel fired two rounds at the elevated shooter. Behind him, the marine could hear Narek cry out in pain and the sound of his armored body hitting the deck. The first round went wide as Samuel ran from his lift to a more robust pylon for cover. It was enough to distract the shooter from finishing Narek, and the merc swept his rifle towards Samuel.

The marine slowly let out his breath as he took his time with the second shot, aiming more carefully at what he could see of the merc from his disadvantaged position. The explosive round struck the merc in the knee and when it detonated the man was left without anything below his thigh.

The wounded merc screamed as he held himself against the rail with one good hand and sprayed full-auto fire at Samuel. The marine dove for the body of the dead Rubicon cor-sec staffer, and grasped the corpse by the shoulder straps of his low-grade bulletproof vest. Samuel felt a round punch through the meat of his calf as he hauled the staffer over him, the vest of the dead man absorbing several more rounds that surely would have ended the marine's life. The rifle clattered to the ground and Samuel peeked out from under the corpse to see that the merc had bled out, his body now hanging limply against the railing.

The marine rushed back to the revolver he'd dropped as Narek, still cursing, punched two hot rounds through the merc who had been engaging the other cor-sec staffer. As Samuel limped over to the main entrance and put his back against the wall, preparing to bushwhack anyone else who came through, he realized that the other staffer had been killed at some point during the exchange. Now only he and Narek remained alive on the cargo deck.

"Anybody comes through that door who ain't our people gets a bullet!" shouted Narek as he wound up his rifle once more to prime a hot round before taking up a defensive position behind a heavy loader, giving him a clear field of fire on the entrance and the dockmaster's platform.

Samuel couldn't hear the comms traffic that Narek could, though he could tell that something had gone wrong on the station.

"We had three shooters try to hit us on the cargo deck, but me and the Reaper dropped 'em, Meridian is firing up the engines now," Narek nodded his head as he listened, and then his expression darkened, "Nah, these guys were way too heavy to ride with that little bastard, must be different outfits on the hunt."

Narek listened again, and then his eyes snapped up to Samuel, and the marine could see the trooper tense.

"I understand, Captain," said Narek as he stood up and walked over to Samuel, his rifle held in one arm and pointed towards the ceiling.

"What's going on in there?" asked Samuel, trying his best not to think about his wife and son and what might have befallen them.

"It's complicated," growled Narek. He lashed out with his mechanical arm and drove the metal fist hard against the marine's temple, the sheer force of the impact rendering Samuel unconscious before his body finished collapsing in a heap on the floor.

The marine blinked himself awake and was dimly aware of being dragged across the deck and up the loading ramp into the *Rig Halo*. People were shouting, though he couldn't tell who, and soon the sounds of their voices became the roar of the ship's engines.

Narek's powerful arms hauled the marine's limp form into a corner where two walls met. It took Samuel a moment to realize he was in the rudimentary medical infirmary on board the Halo. There were enough workplace injuries that medical facilities were a must, only he wasn't sure why he was here. As the marine attempted to get up he realized his hands had been zip-tied together, and he was still woozy from Narek's sucker punch.

The panic at such a cascade of revelations was enough to clear some of the fog in his mind, the rest of it parted like clouds before the sun when Narek stepped aside, allowing Samuel a clear view of the single patient bed in the center of the infirmary.

Time slowed to a crawl as Samuel's eyes took in every minute detail of the scene before him, the ringing in his ears from the thunderous blow to the head making it difficult for him to clearly make out what was being said.

Sura lay on the bed, her duster missing, and blood soaking her body from the chest down. Yanna was using medical scissors to cut away his wife's shirt, slicing it open from the bottom to the collar, and that's when he saw the knife. The handle of a blade jutted up from Sura's chest, and from where Samuel knelt it looked as if it was near her heart, if not close enough that removing the knife without care would damage the vital organ.

Captain Dar leaned in close, his face, streaked with blood and worry, his face right next to Sura's as they held each other's hand. Samuel could see the weak smile on Sura's lips and the light that flickered in her eyes when she opened them to behold the captain.

The marine looked away, knowing that he was an intruder upon what could be her last moments.

It was clear at last who she wanted to spend those moments with.

Samuel's movement caught Narek's eye, and he turned around just enough to move the muzzle of his battle rifle in the marine's general direction to communicate the implied threat.

Behind him, Garn moved up beside the bed and put his hands on Sura to keep her body steady while Yanna held the woman's shoulders. Captain Dar's hand closed around the handle of the knife, and Samuel realized what they were trying to do.

He saw Sura nod and run a hand down Dar's cheek, leaving a smear of blood as it fell onto the table. The captain took a deep breath, jerked the knife out of her body. The instant he did, Sura began to seize, and blood began pumping strongly out of the wound. The knife clattered to the floor as he dropped it, using his other hand to shove the tip of the medic's multi-tool into the wound.

The device reminded Samuel of the device he had carried a lifetime ago when he was the medic for squad Taggart. Right now the device would be flooding Sura's wound with fresh cells, boosting the body's natural coagulants, in addition, to rapidly growing new tissues to heal the wound.

Samuel could see that they'd already hit Sura with several adrenaline stims, and even if she did make it off the table, they would have to seek high-grade medical facilities as soon as possible to keep her heart from burning itself out as it tried to function on whatever parts were not damaged.

After that, the only sound was of Sura's labored breathing as Yanna gave her a sedative so that she wouldn't move accidentally and further damage herself. They strapped her down despite her being unconscious, and one by one everyone left the room except Dar, Narek, and Samuel.

"Who did this?" Samuel finally said, his mind gradually clearing up enough that he was able to get to his feet, pointedly ignoring how Narek kept his gun on him the entire time, the former battle trooper not attempting to hide the threat now that there were fewer witnesses. "And where is my son?"

"Jayce Rinn came to collect a bounty that's been put on your head, he wanted to kidnap and ransom your family to get you," snarled Captain Dar, his former look of concern for Sura replaced swiftly by anger, he clenched his fist and at first it looked as if he was going to attack Samuel, before slamming his fist into the wall instead. "Corbin hauled me and Sura halfway to the ship before I realized I hadn't finished him off. If I ever get my hands on that son of a bitch he is going to die slow."

The captain winced at his now injured hand and began taping it up as he continued.

"Grotto bond recovery agents had the same idea," said Dar as he finished up and turned towards Samuel to pull a data tablet out of his blood-splattered jacket. "Whatever crew tried to hit you on the cargo platform must've just thought they'd come straight for you."

Narek took the offered tablet from Dar and read over it, and Samuel could see the warring reactions of greed and anger as the former battle trooper finished what was there. When the man held it out for Samuel to read, the marine understood why the world had suddenly turned upside down. The Anointed Actuary Kelkis Morturi had issued the acquisition order himself, the very same man that had sat across the negotiating table with Samuel, Lucinda Yulanti, and Wynn Marsters during the Reaper Strike.

Captain Dar spat out a re-telling of the fight on the station, about the bond recovery agents and how they whisked Orion away before he could stop them. Samuel knew that the captain was attempting, in his own way, to apologize for losing the boy. He also knew that the captain would stop at nothing to get him back, not just because he was in love with the boy's mother, but because Orion was part of his crew, part of his family. The marine did not need to hear the captain say such things, and though the man did say them, Samuel wasn't really listening.

The marine's mind was consumed by the gravity of the Anointed's order. For Grotto to make such a bounty public, to float it across all channels corporate and independent, was a tremendous risk of reputation and resources. No expense would be spared in hunting Samuel Hyst to the edges of the universe and beyond. They wanted the Gedra beast that he'd hidden years ago, before leaving Longstride. Until they had him, there would be no rest and no peace for the crew of the *Rig Halo*, for anyone who was an associate of Samuel Hyst, much less his own blood family.

In a flash of harsh clarity, Samuel understood what he needed to do, and hated himself for not having done it years ago when the slavers first appeared. He should have known then that necrospace would never let him go. He was entangled with it to the very core of his being, from derelict ships to alien ruins, and it would follow him no matter how far he ran. Perhaps, for once, he thought to himself, he should charge instead of fleeing. He might not be a Reaper any longer, he might not be much of a father and even less of a husband, but he was a marine, and it was time to act like one.

"Hyst? Are you hearing me? Corbin and I barely survived. Braden is dead and Sura won't last long if we don't get her back to civilization, which will be crawling with mercs and enforcers, " asked Captain Dar, snapping Samuel out of his reverie, "We've got some choices to make here."

"There is no choice, Captain," said Samuel, his voice confident and steady. "Keep your channel active and those recovery agents will reach out. They'll give us a location to meet, and I'll go with them. Sura and Orion become the owners of the Hyst share in the *Rig*. You keep them happy and safe as long as you can."

Narek and Dar looked at each other and then back at Samuel, their faces showing a mixture of surprise and sudden respect.

"I am sorry about Braden. I know the man who issued the order. He will not rest until this matter is resolved, there's no other way," said Samuel, the years of war and toil suddenly feeling heavy upon his shoulders. "Better the recovery agents today than some merc squad tomorrow, and the longer I'm here the more tempted your own people will be to make a move."

"You know an Anointed Actuary?" asked Narek, seemingly oblivious to Samuel's implied suggestion that the former battle trooper would betray his captain's orders and make a run at the bounty himself. "And he knows you?"

"It's been a strange journey getting here," shrugged Samuel, doing his best not to think about the bodies of friends and loved ones lost along the way.

"Goddamn Tango Platoon," growled Narek as he shook his head, though the smile on his face was genuine.

The captain's comms lit up, and Samuel could hear Meridian's voice on the other end.

It was time.

"Let's go get your boy back, Samuel," said Captain Dar as he gestured to Narek to escort the marine out of the room, but then put a hand on Samuel's shoulder to stop him long enough for the captain to cut away the zip ties.

ACQUISITION

Hota 12 was a cold and rugged world, ill-suited to colonization, and with no natural resources beyond the slabs of rock that comprised the majority of the planet surface. On the long-range scanners the planet appeared to be covered in endless snow storms, though upon a second sweep Meridian realized that it wasn't snow, but salt. Braden would have noticed right away, though he was now just another frozen corpse jettisoned into space by the janitorial staff aboard Dagda Station. The distant dwarf star that gave the planet what meager illumination it had did little to warm the world.

A remote planet without utility to any corporate interests and far too inhospitable for even the desperate folk on the Red List. Perfect for conducting an exchange that was best-kept secret.

Meridian piloted the *Halo* to the agreed rendezvous point, struggling against the salt gusts that battered against the hull of the ship. Samuel stood in the cargo bay, flanked on either side by Garn and Narek. Both mercs were in full combat kit, and Samuel was fully aware that they were just as likely to shoot him as they were the Grotto agents if something went badly. No self-respecting mercenary could allow someone else to collect a paycheck for a prize that so many on their side had already bled for.

Samuel had no illusions that he was either leaving Hota 12 alive and in the custody of the Grotto agents or dead with his corpse in storage aboard the *Rig Halo*. Captain Dar would not stop the mercs from doing so, as he had to maintain control by not appearing to be overly weak and sentimental. His troubled relationship, or lack thereof, with Sura Hyst, had done enough damage to his steely reputation as it was.

The *Halo* touched down, and the disembarking lights went green. Captain Dar opened the hatch and immediately the salt began to swirl and collect at the edges of the hatch.

It had been nearly eighteen hours since the fight and their first contact with the Grotto agents and Sura was suffering badly. Samuel had arranged for the agents to provide the captain with additional medical supplies to extend Sura's timeline and give her some hope of surviving the journey back into corporate space.

He wanted to say goodbye, for he did love her, even if the last few years had gone sour. He wanted her to be happy, to be free, and as these thoughts went through his mind Samuel realized that his desires had remained unchanged since the first day she told him she was pregnant. Happiness and freedom for his family. That was why he'd fought and salvaged his way from one end of the universe to the other, to parts beyond and parts in between. His goals had never changed, even if everything else had.

It was some small comfort, a tiny warmth against the cold of Hota 12 as the group of men marched through salt drifts towards the rally point. After nearly ten minutes of trudging over rocks, they saw several dark shapes through the white blur of the storm. One of the figures ignited their orange body lights, and shine off the armor, made them something of a beacon in the salt.

"Hyst," said Narek suddenly, and after he had the marine's attention he tapped his mechanical finger against the war decorations affixed to his armor. "A few of these I got for killing Reapers. I'm thinking about burning 'em off."

Before Samuel could respond Narek looked away, and the moment was lost in the blizzard.

The prospectors and mercenaries drew near, and Samuel saw the three Grotto bond recovery agents standing with guns drawn. He could hear the hum of the force weapons, each charged and ready to unleash devastation. Each of them was no doubt cranked up to lethal settings, as the agents had already suffered wounds of their own, and no chances were being taken.

Samuel could not see any of their faces behind the helmets, though he knew that the fourth person standing next to them, covered head to toe in a hostile enviro-poncho, was Orion. The youth looked up, and though he had on goggles and a re-breather to protect him from the driving salt, Samuel knew it was him. The central armored figure, with a force shotgun, held his hand up to let the oncoming group know to stop.

"Samuel Hyst, identify yourself and take a knee," came the voice of the armored figure, the sound of it carrying through in spite of the storm, amplified as it was by a voice caster.

Samuel did as he was ordered, and knelt down on one knee in the salt drift. Once he did, the armored figure beckoned Orion and walked him at gunpoint until they were beside Samuel. The armored agent looked down, his opaque faceplate all the more menacing in the orange light.

"Orion Hyst has in his possession the medical supplies as we agreed upon," said the agent as he tossed a pair of mag-clamps down to Samuel. "Bind yourself and stand."

Samuel did as he was told, and when he stood he locked eyes with his son as best he could.

They stood like that a moment. The marine dared not make a move to hug the youth, for such a thing might set off shooting. He said nothing for the same reason, only daring to dip his head once, a gesture mirrored by his son.

"Off you go," said the armored man as he pushed Orion with the muzzle of his shotgun, and Orion walked towards Captain Dar and the others.

Samuel watched the boy reach the group, and was happy to see the captain immediately put himself between Orion and the armored agents. The marine looked back at the agent in front of him, who nodded and led Samuel back to where the other two agents still stood with their weapons at the ready.

The marine dared not look back as his son turned and walked away with the mercenaries and prospector captain. The agents seemed to understand and did not prompt him to turn. After a few minutes, the lead agent spoke.

"You have saved Grotto Corporation a tremendous sum in allowing yourself to be apprehended by recovery agents instead of bounty hunters," said the agent as the group began walking towards where their ship presumably waited, "For that, and for your prior service as a Reaper, we corporate citizens thank you. You may continue your journey knowing that Grotto has no lingering interest in the affairs of your family."

"Are we bound for Baen 6, my home world?" asked Samuel as the group walked up the plank into the agent's spacecraft.

"You will be remanded to the wardens on Vex, the nearest Grotto Corporation prison colony," answered one of the other armored agents, the man's voice wheezy as if he struggled to breathe. "Until such time as the Anointed determine your fate."

Samuel felt his pulse pound in his temples, and the surge of adrenaline in his system was fierce. Vex was more of a military installation than a prison colony, where legions of conscripted convicts were forced to fight for the corporation. It appeared that the Anointed had plans for him that extended beyond his knowledge of the beast. Fighting for a penal legion was a death sentence, but one not without some modest use to the corporation, and Grotto was nothing if not masterful in squeezing every last unit of value from human resources.

The agents put him in a small cell near the center of the ship. At first, his thoughts were filled with the loss of his family. The hope that Sura was able to reach a proper hospital in time, regret over missing so much of his son's life, rage at an implacable universe that seemed determined to make him suffer. The corporation that would not leave him alone even after he paid his due.

As time passed, how much of it he wasn't sure, those thoughts of loss transformed into determination. They were on their path, and he was now on his, so it was time to step up.

"Prison it is, then," snarled Samuel to himself as he began what exercises and combat routines he could do in his cramped cell, determined that on the day the cell door opened again he would be ready for whatever fight came next.

"This is the job."

UNTIL THAT DAY

Thank you so much, dear readers, for being patient while this novel reached completion. Samuel Hyst's journey is far from over, and it only gets rougher from here on out. As the series moves past the halfway point and begins the downwards slope towards completion, the stakes will be higher, new characters will emerge, and familiar faces will return to the fore.

Don't miss out!

Visit the website below and you can sign up to receive emails whenever Sean-Michael Argo publishes a new book. There's no charge and no obligation.

https://books2read.com/r/B-A-KCOJ-CFCNC

BOOKS 2 READ

Connecting independent readers to independent writers.

Also by Sean-Michael Argo

Beautiful Resistance
Defiance Pattern
Opposition Shift
Significant Contact

Extinction Fleet
Space Marine Ajax
Space Marine Loki
Space Marine Apocalypse

Necrospace
Salvage Marines
Dead Worlds
Trade War
Ghost Faction
Carrion Duty
Hard Cargo